A Murmuring of Bees

Edited by

Atlin Merrick

Paperback ISBN 9780993513664
ePub ISBN 9780993513671

Published in the UK by Improbable Press Limited
71-75 Shelton Street, Covent Garden, London, WC2H
9JQ
Cover design by Kuuttamo
Cover layout by Tony Herrig

For

Trish

&

For all those who need to know
…it gets better

Contents

Introduction
A Murmuring of Bees

Sherlock Holmes loved bees. Everyone knows that. Don't they?

Well, in the over six hundred thousand words he wrote about the legendary detective, Arthur Conan Doyle mentions Holmes' bees only three times, each mention little more than a single sentence.

I think perhaps we love Sherlock's bees more than Conan Doyle did.

The writers in this anthology certainly do, for all took bees as their starting point, then each wrote a story of love and romance, war and hope, of honey on the tongue or a sting in the tail.

Here there be stories of secret diaries, desperate men, the private language of lovers, and how the meaning of nectar changes depending on who's doing the defining.

Though these stories range from the serene to the silly, though a century separates the times in which some take place, one thing ties them together and that's our love of Sherlock Holmes' love of *bees.*

Whether bees were important to Arthur, they've become important to the fans of his deducing creation. I think we want Sherlock to love bees or honey or hives because it underscores his humanity, because a bee is uncomplicated and bright, and the world in which Sherlock Holmes moves is so often neither of those things.

These stories contain jewels shaped like bees, men named after bees, and beekeeper disguises, bees figure front and centre or sometimes they're as ephemeral as a murmur.

What you'll find in every story is John Watson and Sherlock Holmes helping one another, wanting one another, *loving* one another.

It's that love, that romantic and erotic love between John and Sherlock that's important to Improbable Press. To help encourage a world where such love is seen for the precious thing it is, author and editor profits from *A Murmuring of Bees* will be donated to the It Gets Better Project, whose goal it is to help gay teens understand that, as tough as things might be for them now, *life does get better.*

Atlin Merrick
Editor, *A Murmuring of Bees*
Improbable Press
improbablepress.co.uk

The Memory of Bees
By Verena

Imagine you could understand the murmuring of bees. All the stories about things they have seen. They would tell you about flowers in spring, thunderstorms in summer and maybe, sometimes, about a beloved beekeeper.

But one special hive, one that once belonged to Sherlock Holmes' grandfather, would tell you the story of the pale wingless biped whose skin tasted like honey.

They could not tell you why, again and again, he lay down in the grass next to the apiary, because bees do not know loneliness, or the fierce longing to be touched by a living creature other than oneself.

They would also not be able to tell you why one day Sherlock stopped coming to see them, because they could not know that now there was John Watson, soothing the ache that once plagued the boy. They just missed him and remembered.

The bees *could* tell you about the one time he came back; how they suddenly found the taste of another two-leg on Sherlock's skin. And underlying that, something else. Something almost as sweet as honey. Happiness.

They could not tell you about his farewell words to them because words mean nothing to bees.

But I could.

"I thought you should know," he said, "that it got better."

Then Sherlock smiled and turned away.

"It got *so much better.*"

3

The Overnight Secret
By Darcy Lindbergh

The setting sun blazes across the sky, burning beyond the glass and steel horizon of London and raising shadows out of the narrow alleyways and shuttered buildings below. The darkness is a hiding place, where apathy rubs shoulders with malice, where the empty houses and factories grow teeth between their broken windows, where hope has been forgotten under rot and decay.

Head down, shoulders hunched; it doesn't take much to disappear here. He moves quickly and quietly, carrying his jaw with a weight that tells anyone he might pass to leave him alone. His courage flutters along his veins with cocaine heat and he's sick and tired of waiting.

The basement window breaks with very little effort and he slides through without bothering to clear the glass from the frame. Later, he'll remember about pain, but for now the drugs have dulled everything into a slow buzz in the background, drowned out by the determination to get what he came for.

He finds it in an upstairs bedroom, nestled among some old newspapers in a rough-hewn box with nothing but a cheap clasp to keep it safe, settled on the corner of a dusty bureau. The polished enamel shines in the weak light filtering in through the filthy windows, almost glowing.

It should have been his from the start, he thinks, picking it up with reverence; he imagines he can almost make out his own reflection in the surface and he has his mother's eyes. It should have been his from the start.

There's a creak and the air in the room changes, shifting and moving as a door somewhere else in the house opens and closes. There are footsteps in the hall, coming toward him, almost too soft to hear—but not soft enough.

His fingers close around the handle of the long, wicked knife tucked into his waistband. He has what he came for, and he's not leaving without it.

*

Across London, Sherlock Holmes' eyes fly open with a gasp, stealing the end of his laughter from John Watson's mouth.

"Mm, you like that, do you?" John gives him a lazy, self-satisfied smirk. He pulls back again and pulses his hips shallowly, teasing Sherlock with the suggestion of the next deep drive.

"Might like it better if you did it again," Sherlock huffs, but in the next second he dissolves into breathless giggles and the effect is lost. He hitches his legs higher and writhes against the press of John's hands against his hip bones, trying to entice him, testing John's self-control.

John nips at the corner of his jaw and laughs low and warm against Sherlock's neck. The pump of his hips slows, becomes almost gentle, coaxes a low whine from Sherlock's throat. "You think so?"

The heat in Sherlock's lower belly spins and tightens. He quirks an eyebrow, ready to deliver another cheeky comment, another joke that will set John to laughing against him, but John chooses that exact moment to thrust hard and deep and Sherlock groans instead and suddenly everything is much, much closer. "John, oh god—John *please*—" he manages, brow furrowing and fingers clenching. John finds his mouth again and kisses Sherlock fiercely as he gives, and gives, and gives, and the laughter fades into heaving chests and scrabbling hands and sweat-slick skin.

Then: a gasp and the powerful clench of muscles, shaking, trembling as Sherlock's body unspools itself, followed quickly by unsteady hips and bared teeth and John's stuttering breath of relief.

After, it's quiet. They lay tangled together, the dying light crawling over their bed in shades of rose and lavender as they poke each other in the ribs, giggling with little more than breath and lopsided grins. Their cooling skin sticks together as they murmur to each other about what they might feel like for dinner and whose turn it is to get the shop this week.

"Don't forget the batteries for the clock in the kitchen this time," Sherlock yawns, sinking deeper into the bed. John is warm and close and cosy and the bed smells like them, together, and Sherlock is inclined to let the drowsiness at the edge of his mind take over. "It's still running about ten minutes slow."

John doesn't answer.

Sherlock looks over, and finds John with his eyes closed and his fingers curled loosely on the pillow, breathing deep and even, the tilt of a smile still lingering at the corner of his mouth. The indigo shadows of the sunset catch over the dips and curves of his face, a study in peacefulness and tranquility.

Something hot and dazzling and sweet rises in Sherlock's chest: words that are too big for Sherlock's mouth, for the laughter and the adrenalin and the overall newness of a bed that's not quite *theirs*, that used to be Sherlock's alone. John's eyelashes flutter briefly against his cheek and a secret is born under Sherlock's breastbone and held there like a breath, cautious and uncertain.

Sherlock has never really thought before about love.

When he met John, barely six months ago, the only things Sherlock knew about love were the things he learned from crime scenes: that it sours into venom and vengeance. That it ignites into jealousy and rage. That it sprawls its victims out in their own blood as they ignore the wounds.

And then there was John, discarded by the army for the bullet hole they'd put in him, a soldier and doctor without something to fight for, something to protect. Sherlock had been looking for a flatmate and instead got a partner and a friend, and then, both slowly and suddenly at once, something deeper, something more. Something *intimate*. Casual hands on shoulders and smiles across the table had turned into fingers dipping under shirt hems and into trouser waistbands and smiles they could taste from each other's mouths.

Now John is nuzzling closer into Sherlock's shoulder, humming faintly through sleep and dream, and Sherlock is in love with him. They argue and they laugh and they tease, and they move around each other, move with each other, like they always have done. They go out into the streets and up against the underworld, and afterward they come home and fall together, heady with danger and adventure and near-misses, but he doesn't think either of them ever really intended for it to be serious and Sherlock *loves* him.

John sleeps on, unaware, and Sherlock swallows against the feeling rising in his throat. What they have is good, he thinks. What they have is just alchemy, excitement mixed with victory and warm bodies, and

Sherlock doesn't want to ruin it by trying to make it into something it's not.

He closes his eyes and curls his fingers around John's wrist, feeling for the beat of his heart, wondering if it ever calls his name.

Somewhere in the flat, a mobile rings.

*

The house is old and so is everything in it, the dust and the faded curtains and the smell of mould and withering lilac. The rooms are too dark, even with the artificial electric lights the Met has brought in. There's a distinct feeling of abandonment and decay that makes everyone speak with hushed tones, as if the house itself is a mausoleum built specifically to house the dead man on the bedroom floor.

Sherlock kneels by the body and tries to focus. John hovers in his peripheral vision, never far away, silhouetted against the grimy window as he looks out onto the street. The twilight is gorgeous on him and Sherlock can still feel his phantom touch in his thighs and arse and shoulders, in the stretch and pull of sore muscles.

Focus. Pay attention. The body on the floor, not the body by the window. What does this body tell him? What does the blood tell him, the wounds, the violence?

"Personal," he mutters under his breath. "Incredibly violent, far more violent than necessary. Fifteen, sixteen stab wounds? Definitely personal." He looks up at Lestrade, hovering in the dark doorway. "What do we know about him?"

"Not much," Lestrade says. "Name's Bill Sheffield. Nothing yet on any family connections—the neighbours say he kept to himself mostly, didn't think he had a job or a girlfriend, none of that sort of thing. A few of them thought he'd inherited this house from his parents, said there might be a younger brother. We're trying to find him now."

Sherlock hums and rocks back onto his heels, taking in the larger scene. He wishes the Met had thought to bring him in first, to let him see the room uninterrupted; the footprints in the dust, now marred by police and forensics and all their equipment, would have told the story, would have let him arrange the killer and the victim back into the space and see how they moved around each other. There'll be pictures somewhere, of course, but it's never as good, never as accurate as the real thing.

"Sherlock, look at this."

Across the room, John stands in front of the bureau by the window, staring at a shoddy wooden box settled on the corner, the expression on his face lost in shadow. Sherlock gets to his feet. "What is it?"

"I don't know, but there are finger marks in the dust here, on the lid," John says. He glances over his shoulder and gives Sherlock an excited grin. "Recent ones."

The artificial lights are directed at the centre of the room, leaving the corners dark and making the marks hard to see, but the movement of fingers in the dust, opening and closing the lid, is fairly obvious. The box seems too insecure, too graceless to hold anything of importance, but the marks are fresh and a dead body is only a few steps away.

"Lestrade, gloves, please," Sherlock says absently, holding his hand out behind him. A pair of latex gloves are pressed into his palm and he snaps them on, meeting John's gaze. John smiles back, his excitement lingering

10

around the corners of his eyes, and he nods in encouragement.

Sherlock loves these moments, these on-the-verge-of-something, about-to-discover-something moments, the anticipation, the tension. He loves the way John loves them too, the way John loves the mysteries and the curiosities, the questions they meet with in the work they've built a life out of together, and there's a sudden surge of warmth and exhilaration in Sherlock's belly.

John is tailor-made for this life that Sherlock leads, and this life is tailor-made for John in return, and Sherlock sees a future together that thrives between the cases, feasts on adrenalin and triumph and the satisfaction, and he wants to reach over and kiss John right then.

But it's not the time, and it's not the place, and there isn't room in their life or their relationship for the eager heat in Sherlock's chest, and he has to look away.

He takes a deep breath and opens the box.

"Newspaper?" John says, brow furrowing in disappointment. "Just—crumpled up newspaper?"

"Yes, but look," Sherlock breathes. His gloved fingers trace along the papers. "There's a cavity. Something was kept in here. The killer must have taken it, whatever it was."

John hums, watching Sherlock's hands trace out the space. "They came for this, then, not to kill Sheffield. Just the wrong place at the wrong time?"

"The wrong person at the wrong place at the wrong time, more like." Sherlock looks back at the body, the blood underneath it beginning to crust black with dirt and stillness and the heat from the artificial lights. "The killer came for this, but it wasn't a matter of just trying to get away with this thing. This murder—the violence—the killer was angry, vengeful even, they didn't just want to kill Sheffield—"

"They wanted to make Sheffield pay for having it," John finishes, understanding lighting in his eyes. "Sheffield inherited this house. The younger brother."

"We've not found him yet," Lestrade interrupts, stepping in closer to get a look at the box. "But one of the neighbours remembered him. His name is Adam, Adam Sheffield." He tips his head toward the space in the newspapers. "What could that have been, d'you think?"

Sherlock snaps off the gloves and throws John a wink across the bureau. "I guess we'll find out when we find Adam Sheffield, won't we?"

*

The weight of it tucked into his jacket, pressed against his stomach, sends a thrill up his spine. He's got it, he's got it, he's got it, and nobody can take it away from him now.

He finds a few old candle stubs in the corner of the room and lights them with trembling fingers and a single match. His blood is starting to calm now, to slow down inside his veins, and he can see it all over his hands. He picks up an old t-shirt and wipes at the stains and tells himself that if the t-shirt can't get his hands clean, his hands won't get his prize dirty.

The broken window panes don't stop the wind from coming in as a storm moves over London. Clouds gather and build, smoky purple and grey in the blue-black, blotting out the moonlight. This part of the city is always dark, and the candles stutter against the deepening night, fearful and flickering like his pulse in his chest.

He looks over his shoulder a few more times to make sure he's alone, and then he reaches into his jacket and brings it out.

It's like holding summertime in his hands, freshly cut grass and the buzz of the dragonflies, countryside gullies laced with streams and tall rushes. It's his mother laughing in the sun, kissing a skinned knee, holding his hand. It's the way things were when things were easy, before the ancient musty house, before the city, before the drugs.

The pink flowers seem to sway across the turquoise backdrop of his mother's jewelry box, and the tiny yellow and black bumblebee crawls across it all, its mother-of-pearl wings flickering in the candlelight.

She kept seashells in it, instead of jewelry, even after the summers in the country had faded into memory, even after they came to the city with all its screaming lights and angry people, even after there wasn't any money anymore for treasures. She kept pictures of them, and locks of hair, baby teeth and second-prize ribbons, things they brought home as tiny offerings, trying to be chosen, trying to be kept.

Always more of Billy than of him.

He swallows down the sour memories of trying to earn her adoration, desperate to make it into the box, desperate to be prized. His fingers twitch over the clasp, wondering if there is even any of him left.

Outside, it begins to rain, an uneven rhythm that steals through the broken windows like a warning. A pink-tinged fingerprint begins to dry across the enameled image of a cherry blossom, unnoticed, as the wind blows the candles out.

*

13

Midnight is a lightning strike, streets drenched with rain and skies black with fury. Sherlock leads, sneaking around corners and up alleys. John follows close behind, every inch the soldier with his shoulders pulled back and his eyes turned hard with fearlessness. London may be their city, their stronghold, but not all its denizens are glad of a detective in their midst.

Sherlock grins against the storm, savouring the moment.

This is what they do, and this is how they do it best: sliding into the places they aren't wanted, finding the people that don't want to be found, black jackets and dark doorways holding them close and hiding them from anxious eyes.

This is where they found themselves wanting, needing, hearts pounding and palms sweating and the air thick with lust, kisses full of mischievous grins and daring tongues, Sherlock's back scraping against a wall with every rolling thrust.

Then they'd brought it home, kept it close, slowed the kisses down into something delicate and let the adrenalin slip away into sleeping.

Now Sherlock has confused himself, let himself settle in too deep, and the heat of the love in his throat stings against the knowledge that it was never meant to be like this. It isn't supposed to be about love. It isn't made for love. It's made out of them, and they're made for the razor's edge, danger and fire and crashing together.

"You all right?" John's voice, low and serious, cuts into his thoughts. Sherlock swallows and shakes away the rain drops catching in his eyelashes.

"Nearly there," he says, dodging the question. He shouldn't be thinking about it, not right now; only the uncomfortable newness of the feeling keeps bringing it back to mind. They're on a case, on the chase, on the prowl, and if he can't get his head in the game, he's going to get them both killed and love would have nothing to do with it.

Adam Sheffield is an elusive sort, though fortunately not quite as elusive as his brother. It has only taken a single mug shot—an arrest for possession of narcotics several years ago that never got off the ground—and a few well-directed questions for some of the homeless Sherlock knows down in Vauxhall to get a nod of recognition and an address.

As they creep around one last corner, the house looms up ahead of them. The rain seems to be beating it down: the roof is half caved in, the door left half-open where the slanting frame would no longer let it fit, as though it's collapsing in on itself.

"There's no telling whether he'll run or fight," Sherlock reminds John quietly as they get closer, "but I doubt he'll just give up. Are you ready?"

"Ready," John says, his eyes glimmering against the rain, darting over the house, checking possible exits, looking for shadows in the windows. He's beautiful, soaked to the skin and steaming with anticipation, his hands flexing against his thighs, and in the next instant Sherlock can't resist. He leans in and presses a hard kiss against John's mouth, feels the smirk on John's lips as he kisses back.

"Ready," Sherlock confirms as he pulls away, and then he darts up the front steps and through the open front door, John close on his heels and laughing under his breath.

*

15

He runs.

He runs and they give chase, faces serious but hearts pounding fast with glee and it feels like flying, racing after him, closing in. Sherlock's legs are longer but John is quicker, and they keep pace, almost shoulder-to-shoulder, eyes intent on the figure in front of them and yet always aware of each other, always sharing in it with one another even when they don't speak, don't look.

Sheffield is coming down off a high, stumbling over shoes that are too worn down and a body that moves like it's held together by string, his hands full of something shockingly colourful in the grime and grit of the deserted streets. He has desperation on his side, but not much else, and Sherlock and John have built their lives on ending the chase.

The rain slows to a drizzle and then a mist, shrouding the streetlamps with fog and turning the sky overhead purple like a bruise where the clouds begin to break. Sheffield runs, and runs, a ten-minute lead whittling away to five, and two, and then there's a split second of hesitation and John bursts forward.

It's quick, from there: John pushes his weight into Sheffield's shoulders and brings him down headfirst, and Sheffield twists and yells but doesn't fight—he's too focused on the vivid thing in his hands, on keeping it from smashing along the ground. Sherlock is right behind them, though, and it's the work of an instant to slip smoothly past John, around him, both of them already anticipating the other's movement, to get control of his hands. They're sticky with blood, dried in streaks, and Sherlock knocks aside the thing he's holding to pull them back and handcuff his wrists together.

John sits back, straddling Sheffield's waist to keep control of him while he smiles up at Sherlock, almost wild with victory and excitement. Their eyes meet and lock and they sink into one another, without touching, without saying a word, and Sherlock can feel the breadth and joy of John's grin on his skin as easily as if John had leaned over and pressed his mouth against him.

John works his mobile out of his denims pocket, no doubt to dial 999 and probably Lestrade, ignoring Sheffield as he thrashes and shouts. Sherlock ignores him as well, and instead turns his attention to the box that has clattered out of Sheffield's grasp.

It's only about as big as Sherlock's two hands, but the box is undoubtedly a work of art, ornately enameled with opalescent cherry blossoms and a bumblebee in the corner, fitted together with gold outlines. Sherlock traces over a wing with his fingertips. Clearly cherished, clearly precious, and clearly what was hidden away in the crude, hand-made box on Bill Sheffield's bureau.

Such a small thing to kill for.

"It's mine," Adam Sheffield howls from beneath John's iron grip. "It's *mine*, it should always have been mine. I was the one what found it for her."

"Your mother?" Sherlock asks. He crouches down and holds it in front of Sheffield's eyes. "You killed your brother for a trinket box that used to be your mother's?"

Sheffield snaps his teeth at Sherlock, mimicking a bite, before John's hand closes roughly around the back of his neck, just tight enough to be sure that he won't be able to reach Sherlock. "He never should have had it. It was mine."

"It's evidence in your brother's murder, now." John has already moved on, absently inspecting Sheffield's wrists and shoulders for injuries he might have sustained in the fall, keeping him secure.

Sherlock feels around the edge and finds the latch, clicking the box open. He pulls out a worn, sepia-toned photograph of a beautiful woman and a small child: a small child with the same snub nose as a dead body on a slab across London, totally unlike the nose Sheffield is currently rubbing against the concrete.

"Envy," he realises, holding up the picture. "When you love someone so much, and you want them to love you back, but you can never quite be sure if they'll ever love you the same way you love them."

"Had to earn my spot in the box," Sheffield confirms. The fight has mostly gone out of him now; he's nearly crying.

Sherlock understands, and his heart clenches painfully in his chest. His spot in John's life is so dependent on the race, the chase, the adventure, and he understands. "Sometimes love makes a weapon of us," he says. "It sharpens up our fears and sends us into battle against the uncertainty. And we end up murdering our brothers for trinket boxes."

Sherlock shakes his head to clear it. He's conflating; being almost unforgivably inaccurate; he needs to move on. He looks over and finds that John's smile has faded, and he's looking up at Sherlock with wide eyes.

"Love isn't the same thing as fear," John says, terribly softly. "Sherlock, you don't need—don't you know—?"

Then there's a siren and the alley spins into a blue and red kaleidoscope as the police descend, and John doesn't finish.

What they have is enough, Sherlock tells himself as they drag themselves back into the flat, exhausted and exhilarated, dripping onto the carpets, helping each other strip off their wet clothes. He's almost mad at himself for not being grateful. They have good soft moments, tender moments, delicacies and extravagances with one another. At home. Curled up together on the sofa watching documentaries. Coming up behind one another and resting their faces between shoulder blades, along the backs of necks.

Things will even out eventually, Sherlock knows. The hot insistent feeling in his chest will fade into no more than playful affection and physical desire, the way it ought to be.

The thought makes him a little cold-shouldered though. When John slips into bed beside him for the night, he pretends to be asleep, and then feels put out when John doesn't curl around him.

*

It's soft and warm and the sun behind Sherlock's eyelids is pink and hazy. John's arm is a solid weight around his middle and he's not sure what woke him— the stretch of sleep-soft muscles, or the answering slide of John's hand over his belly. He shifts and opens his eyes; the sun is still soft and early, probably just past dawn. They should be asleep for hours yet, but John's arm tightens around his waist and pulls him a little bit closer.

"Morning," he rasps, rubbing his nose over Sherlock's shoulders, just below the nape of his neck, before pressing a light kiss there. His fingers draw an idle circle on Sherlock's stomach.

God, but Sherlock loves him.

The thought makes Sherlock's head dip away in embarrassment, and the arm around his waist suddenly feels like a trap. The things he said last night swarm through his mind like locusts, sharp and buzzing. He tries to scoot away, but John doesn't move his hand, and instead he kisses Sherlock's shoulders again.

"Don't," John says. "Stay."

His arm is loose enough that Sherlock could leave if he really wanted to, but John continues to nuzzle at his skin, pressing kisses up the line of his neck, chaste and careful instead of sensual. "Stay," he repeats. "Stay here with me."

Sherlock doesn't relax, but he stays.

The honeyed light of dawn filters through Mrs Hudson's lace curtains, dappling the bed in pink and gold. It's quiet the way only London is quiet at dawn, with the low rumble of busses and lorries, the gentle hum of a city that never truly stops turning toward the day. John continues to stroke his fingers over Sherlock's belly, encouraging him to loosen and let go of the tension in his limbs.

"Shh," John murmurs, even though Sherlock hasn't made a noise. "Shh."

It's too early and neither of them have had enough sleep, but John waits and soothes and hums in the back of his throat, a noise that would be a reassurance if it gave way to words. He comforts Sherlock without even knowing what he's comforting him for, without asking, without needing to know, and Sherlock loves him so much it presses at his breastbone and clogs up his mouth and it *hurts*.

"John," Sherlock whispers. His voice cracks. "John, I."

There's a pause and Sherlock doesn't know what to say. He wants to tell John about the feeling in his chest, to apologise, and he wants to tell John that John has to go and that he can't come back to Sherlock, not like this. He wants to say the words out loud and he wants to ask if John could ever say them back, but it's pathetic and mawkish and ridiculous, to put that expectation onto John.

Then John props himself up on one elbow so he can see Sherlock's face. He leans in and brushes his lips over Sherlock's cheek. "Sherlock," John whispers, "I think you've got the wrong idea."

Sherlock closes his eyes in rejection and defeat. Of course John would know, of course he would.

John rubs his nose along Sherlock's cheekbone, following when Sherlock tries to shift away. "You've got the wrong idea," he repeats. "I think you've totally missed the point." He kisses at the corner of Sherlock's unyielding mouth, which seems needlessly cruel and Sherlock squeezes his eyes shut a little tighter. "And I think it's my fault, a bit, and I'm sorry. I should have made myself clear at the very start."

"It's fine," Sherlock croaks, "I understood."

"No, you didn't," John says, sad and almost disbelieving. "Because I love you, and you don't seem to know about it."

Sherlock is perfectly, utterly still. He wants desperately to crack his eyes open and look long and hard at the expression on John's face, but fears the lie he might find there.

John leans in closer and kisses Sherlock's temple. "I love you," he whispers. A kiss to Sherlock's jaw. "I love you." A kiss to the side of his nose. "I love you. Sherlock, breathe."

The breath comes in shaky and hot and Sherlock scrambles to roll onto his back. John catches him, pulls him close, finally finds Sherlock's mouth with his and kisses him, deeply and softly at once, almost unbearably gentle but for the words Sherlock can still taste on his tongue. John kisses him like he *means it*, like the idea that Sherlock might have doubted it burns him, scalds him through to his marrow, solemn and hushed and tender.

One more chaste kiss, and then John draws back, watching, waiting. When Sherlock doesn't open his eyes right away he kisses Sherlock's forehead, both his eyelids, the tip of his nose.

"I do love you," Sherlock says, in awe of the sound of the words in his own voice. He finally opens his eyes and looks. John looks back at him, his own eyes crinkled at the corners and maybe a little wet, and he reaches up to touch, rubbing his thumb over Sherlock's cheek like Sherlock is something precious and cared for and yes, impossibly but irrefutably loved. "John."

John laughs, soft and peaceful, and this time when he kisses Sherlock it feels like the dawn cresting over the city, awash with gold and hope and the promise of all the days stretched out before them, endlessly moving together and into the light.

Tales from the River Bank
By Kim Le Patourel

"Let's walk," Sherlock says as they exit the tower block into the pre-dawn gloom of the street.

John doesn't say a word, simply falls into step. Sherlock notes the way John is clenching and unclenching his hands, his furious focus on the pavement beneath his feet, the hitch in his stride, and he fervently wishes that—just this once—he hadn't woken John to accompany him.

When they reach Hungerford Bridge—Sherlock still can't bring himself to refer to it as Jubilee Bridge—he hesitates for a second then turns right, taking them along the south bank of the river rather than towards home. John doesn't appear to notice.

"Do you want to talk?" Sherlock risks, a moment later.

"What is there to say?" John's voice is harsh, overloud despite the fact that he's still not raised his head.

"That family are all dead." A little quieter.

"But you solved it." His voice drops further.

"There's nothing more."

John stumbles and Sherlock fights every one of his instincts to reach out and steady him. John does not want his help. Correction, John does want his help, just not that sort of help. Physical manifestations of mental distress do not have physical cures. John needs support of a different kind.

A memory surfaces, from years ago; Mycroft finding him under the dining room table and squeezing under too—map in one hand and a book of poems in the other. Sherlock can't remember now what he'd been hiding from. He can remember the poem, though, and his attempts at composing a suitable tune to set it to.

He's humming before he realises it, the swish and sigh of the river to his left providing a perfect accompaniment.

"That's nice," John says. He's walking a little closer to Sherlock now. "I've not heard it before."

"It's one of mine." Sherlock hums another few phrases then looks down at John. "One of the first things I ever tried to compose. A Song of the Thames. A River's Tale."

John looks up in surprise. Sherlock can't tell if it's the mention of the river or his childhood that's piqued John's interest and, for once, he doesn't mind not being sure. He just keeps talking.

"I've always loved this river. From when I was very young," he says, turning towards the balustrade and leaning on it, forearms flat on the wide top, the ceramic and glass bee cufflinks John gave him for his birthday glinting in the light of the street lamp.

John steps up too, but rests against him, rather than the stone. Sherlock swallows, keeps his face pointing out toward the glimmering water as he resumes speaking.

"I thought it was invincible. Stopped for nothing, answered to no-one, saw everything."

There's a brief huff from John. Sherlock doesn't turn. Instead he takes a breath and softly sings:

"Twenty bridges from Tower to Kew
Wanted to know what the river knew
For they were young and the Thames was old
And this is the tale that the river told—"

"It's Kipling. Mycroft brought it to me one day. Showed me the bridges on a map and where the different sections of the poem happened as he read. Mummy was less than impressed when I spent the next six months re-enacting my favourite bit."

He starts to sing again:

"And I remember like yesterday
The earliest Cockney who came my way,
When he pushed through the forest that lined the Strand,
With paint on his face and a club in his hand.
He was death to feather and fin and fur.
He trapped my beavers at Westminster.
He netted my salmon, he hunted my deer,
He killed my heron off Lambeth Pier.
He fought his neighbour with axes and swords,
Flint or bronze, at my upper fords."

Sherlock sneaks a sideways glance at John. He's staring out over the water, face blank, but the haunted look is receding and one corner of John's mouth is tilting upwards a little.

"I don't think next door's cat ever forgave me for trying to give it a starring role in one production…as the beaver."

This time John actually snorts and then his arm snakes round Sherlock's waist.

"I used to watch the Helmand River."

Sherlock doesn't move. Doesn't dare do more than breathe shallowly, for fear John might not continue. For long minutes there's no sound but the soft splashing of the Thames lapping at the bank below them and the purr of distant cars as the city slowly begins to wake.

"I'd watch the water, try to lose my thoughts in the eddies when sleep just wouldn't come. It didn't happen often but…"

John stops, left hand tightening on Sherlock's waist. Then he shifts his weight forward so that while he's still pressed against Sherlock he's leaning on the balustrade too, right arm next to Sherlock's, right hand clenched into a fist.

"I shouldn't have done it. But the boy ran up to us, grabbed my sleeve, begged for help and I…I couldn't just ignore him, or the cries I could hear through the open door. I thought they might overlook it, seeing as how I saved both mother and baby. The father was grateful. Came to the compound the next day with a loaf of bread for me. It might have been that bread that tipped the balance in the end. I don't know. I never understood how they thought… Whatever it was, it was enough."

John slams his fist against the stone.

"The entire family, Sherlock. All ten of them. Slaughtered. Just because I'd been in their house."

"You found them."

It's a statement, not a question but John answers anyway.

"Yes. They'd been dead a couple of days by that point. Just like…" John jerks his head in the approximate direction of the crime scene. "We never patrolled the same route twice in a row or we might have found them sooner. Not that it would have mattered. The bastards that did it made sure they died quickly, at least. The only thing I could have done was not have gone inside in the first place. I…I wished I hadn't. Still do. At least that way only two of them would have died."

Sherlock doesn't say any of the words that are chasing around his head; that John wasn't responsible for the warped justice the Taliban meted out; that John

26

wouldn't have known he'd saved the rest of the family by sacrificing the mother and child; that John wouldn't be John, wouldn't have been able to live with himself, if he'd walked away. Instead he takes John's fist in both his own hands, lifts it to his mouth and presses a kiss to the knuckles.

John makes an indistinct noise in the back of his throat and lets his head fall onto Sherlock's shoulder. Sherlock gently returns their hands to the balustrade and for long minutes there is just the shushing of the river and the soft drag of their breathing, John's still a little faster than Sherlock's.

Then John unclenches his fist and moves his hand, resting it lightly on Sherlock's wrist, thumb circling the bee cufflink in a way that makes Sherlock's throat close up.

"Sing it all for me?" John whispers as the first rays of dawn set the Thames aglow.

Sherlock swallows, and then he does.

A Sting On the Tail
By Verity Burns

"How much longer?"

"Almost done, Sherlock. Just hold still, will you?"

"I *am* holding still."

"No, you're not. You're shifting about as if you've got ants in your pants."

"Well, they'd hardly be bothering me at the moment, would they? You've got my pants round my ankles!"

"I've only lowered them the bare minimum, so unless your ankles have mysteriously relocated to your hips, you're making a big fuss about nothing. Now hold *still!*"

"I'm *uncomfortable!*"

"Well, how do you think the poor bee felt, seeing your great arse descending towards it? Look before you sit!"

"I…what?"

"There! All done. Now just stay put for a second and I'll get a cold compress."

"…John?"

"There we go—that should help."

"John, what do you mean by 'great'?"

"What?"

"You said my arse was 'great'. What did you mean?"

"Oh! Well, I guess I meant…not small."

"Right."

"Sorry."

"It's fine. Are you done?"

"Yes."

"Thank you. Tea?"

"Never mind tea. What is with you lately?"

"How do you mean?"

"The odd questions. The sudden physical shyness. You're being weird."

"My apologies."

"I don't want your apologies. I want to know…well, what if I'd meant *great* arse instead of *great* arse?"

"I…"

"Yes?"

"I want…I mean, I… "

"Let me spell it out, Sherlock. Friends or lovers. Which?"

"…"

"…"

"Both."

(This is the first of seven 221Bs in this anthology. An homage to John and Sherlock's Baker Street address, a 221B is a story of two hundred and twenty-one words, with the final word beginning with B. - Editor)

Prick
By Meredith Spies

I.

As far as visits to A&E went, this one was far more interesting than usual. His doctor was shouting, "It's a prick, Geoffrey! A *prick*! A red, swollen, prick!"

Sherlock would never admit it, but he would have laughed had he not been dying.

Geoffrey, a red-faced, round-bodied man who towered over Doctor-Watson-nice-to-meet-you-well-perhaps-not-under-these-circumstances, made a sound somewhere between a growl and a bark. "It. Is. A. Bee. Sting."

"*Prick.*"

Geoffrey, whom Sherlock deduced to be Doctor Watson's superior (to be fair the deduction was quite easy, since Geoffrey had said "Watson, I am your superior!" immediately upon Watson dragging him into the exam room, but Sherlock's head was so swimmy, he didn't care to split hairs on the nature of his deduction), made the growl-bark sound again. "Bee sting allergy protocol, Watson. So help me, if I see you've ordered any extra tests from the lab." Geoffrey's threat went unspoken, but even Sherlock knew what a potential sacking sounded like.

Watson ordered extra tests from the lab.

Sherlock was barely conscious, the taste of vomit sharp and heavy in his mouth, pulse throbbing in his ears, when Doctor Watson leaned over him to murmur, "Poison. I knew it. You're being transported to University Hospital."

Sherlock nodded, squeezing his eyes shut and resolving to invite the doctor to move to 221B.

II.

It took two weeks for Sherlock to become annoyed with Watson's presence. Watson was an itch on the bottom of his foot when he was wearing boots and thick socks. He was the nagging feeling the stove's been left on, when Sherlock was two zones from home and stuck in traffic. He was...he was *humming*. "Do you mind?"

Watson paused in his collating of case notes. "Not in the slightest." He smiled and resumed his collating.

Collating.

Who collates, really?

Sherlock stalked to the desk and towered over Watson. "You're *humming.*"

"Well spotted. No wonder you're a detective." His smile was a curly thing, pushing his cheeks to dimple and his eyes to crinkle. "Regretting asking an unemployed doctor to live with you now?"

Sherlock opened his mouth to say *yes, very much so* but what came out was "Don't be daft, Watson. Your help is invaluable to me. Now. Where are the notes on the McKinnon case?"

"There are no notes, Sherlock." Watson stood, but Sherlock did not step back. "McKinnon poisoned you. The Yard is looking for him. No notes."

They were close, almost touching. Interest stirred in Sherlock's belly, pushed through his veins. "Watson?"

"I..." Watson licked his own lips, nodded. They had moved in orbit around one another for weeks, gravity pulling them closer together. "Yes," Watson breathed.

III.

Love, Sherlock decided, staring at his bedroom ceiling. Definitely love. Trust being poisoned and almost dying to end like this. He closed his eyes, feeling Watson's tongue move down his belly in his self-created dark. He groaned, full-throated and unabashed, when Watson's mouth finally closed over the head of his cock, tongue swirling lavishly across Sherlock's leaking slit. McKinnon's capture by the Yard had merited Sherlock a tight embrace from Watson, which, in turn, had merited a surprisingly persistent and obvious erection from Sherlock. Which...well. Sherlock opened his eyes to look down at Watson. This. This had been the ultimate result. He sank the fingers of one hand into Watson's hair and held tight, not pushing but guiding. Watson hummed (*always humming!*) approval, cupping Sherlock's bollocks and tugging gently. Sherlock's hips arched and his breath stuttered. "Watson...*John*..."

"I know, love," Watson...John...murmured against Sherlock's thigh.

Sherlock's release was swift and messy and perfect, 'love' echoing in his thoughts and rattling down his bones. He curled into Wa—John's side. "I never thought I'd be glad of being poisoned."

"I never thought I'd be glad of being sacked."

"I never thought I'd be glad of sharing my life."

"I never thought I'd have someone to share with."

Sherlock huffed a laugh. "I'm glad you never thought it was a bee."

The Secret Diary of Dr John Watson MD
By Kerry Greenwood

Ashmolean number 991 - 4027 - SH - closed archive

This document is a small brown leather-covered notebook, found in a strongbox beneath the floor of a cottage in Sussex where it is believed by some scholars that Sherlock Holmes and Doctor Watson spent their retirement. The box also contained various legal documents, including a will (list attached), several military medals, a pair of opal cufflinks, ten gold sovereigns, a phial containing a seven percent solution of cocaine, and a syringe in a shagreen case. Authorities believe that the box was buried and then later forgotten, as the later owners of the cottage cleared out all the possessions and especially written material relating to the famous detective and donated it to this institution in 1938. Some of it was lost to enemy action. Some of the collection is now displayed in the Sherlock Holmes Museum in Baker Street, London. The handwriting has been authenticated as belonging to Dr John Watson by Dr J Somerville, the noted Holmes scholar. The contents are now the subject of heated scholarly debate. This is a closed archive. Special permission from the Director must be obtained to gain access to it, and it may not be copied, summarised, or photographed for any but the purposes of private study.

It begins without any date or even mention of a day. But it must, from internal evidence, date to March 21st 1895, when the impending trial of Oscar Wilde for Gross Indecency was reported in the *Times.* In style and sentence construction it matches Dr Watson's usual work.

*

I came home from the club late, tired, a trifle bosky, and half disgusted by the attentions of the young man for whose time and skill I had paid.

Since Mary died I had no wish to try for another female companion. She had been a perfect specimen of her gender. I preferred, for relief, and perhaps to ease my burning, unrequitable desire for my friend, to visit the discreet club I had attended as a captain. We were all military men, all of us with so much to lose that no guilt-ridden wretch was likely to peach on us.

I went there when I desired to be, for a little while, caressed and embraced and loved. For a fee, of course. The club was respectable. We did not employ boys. All of our young men were clean, well fed, well paid, comely and discreet. They were charming and kind to me and my broken heart and my long held, long denied love for my companion.

I had moved back to 221B and it was as comfortable as before. Mrs Hudson was gratifyingly pleased to see me, and I flattered myself not just for the security of the rent. Sherlock, who had ample means, used often to forget to pay.

"Take it from the brass bowl on the mantelpiece," he would tell her, waving that long white hand. And there might be cash in the bowl, or there might not. Mrs Hudson had no means of knowing.

I did examine her rickety knee and prescribed some massage and treatments which she said did her a lot of good.

But she was always a kind woman.

And since I had returned, I was a tired man. Nothing amused me, particularly. I ate and slept and drank and visited the whores when I could stay away no longer, but something inside me seemed to be decelerating, like a watch with a defective mainspring. I was aging, slowing down, on the road to senescence and death. And I didn't really mind.

"Come, Watson, I have ordered us a tidy little supper," exclaimed Holmes, leaping up from his couch. "And some rather good wine. You have drunk, but you have not eaten."

Thus spoke the man who knew everything. He was right. I had not eaten.

I hung up my coat, doffed my hat, and went into my bedroom to wash my hands, take off my collar and boots, and assume my slippers and dressing gown. It had been a cool night outside, and the flat seemed warm and cosy and comforting by contrast.

Holmes 'little supper' was a collection of excellent dishes from a very expensive Italian restaurant, perhaps Sardi's. The wine was a Chateaux Margaux. I wondered what we were celebrating. It all smelled very good and I was suddenly hungry.

Holmes helped me to some partridge and poured me a glass of the red wine. Then he held up his glass in a toast.

"To friendship," he said.

I raised my own and drank to friendship. I picked at the pheasant with shallots and almonds. It was excellent. I tried the artichokes.

Holmes was up to something. He was fidgeting with those long fingers, as though he was longing to pick up his violin. He tasted the poulet royale, commented on its piquancy, and drank more wine.

Then he rose and locked first the outer door, so that no one could get in from the street, and then the door to our own apartment, so that not even Mrs Hudson could gain entry. I raised an eyebrow. What had he to say that must not be overheard by even our innocent landlady? The shutters were across the windows. No one could hear from the outside. It must be a case of the utmost secrecy.

He dropped the keys in his dressing gown pocket and I ate some more partridge, waiting for the exposition of the problem. But Holmes began talking about les Grands Vins, something he does sometimes to cover another train of thought. I always get lost around the varieties of Bordeaux, and in any case, I was tired. I was always tired these latter days.

"Watson!" he said sharply, and I jerked awake. In my defence, I had heard the lecture before. Several times.

"Holmes?" I asked.

"Did you so much as glance at the *Times* today?"

"I did," I replied. "To what item would you draw my attention?"

"Oscar Wilde is to stand trial for Gross Indecency," he said.

"Always was a fool, lounging around at the Cafe Royale, flaunting his...predilections for all to see."

"Agreed," said Holmes. He drank more wine. "But these predilections are shared by many innocent people. This Criminal Law Amendment Act will give the police free reign, and make every blackmailer rub his vile hands with joy."

"Yes," I agreed. "It will be terrible."

"Your club," he started. Then he stopped and gulped Margaux. He never drank this much. "That club," he went on. "The one you attended tonight."

"Yes?" I quavered. I had no idea he knew I was an invert. I had gone to such lengths to hide it from him. The idea of successfully hiding anything like that from Sherlock Holmes should have made me smile, but I was horrified. I dreaded his reaction to this discovery of my depravity.

"You must not go there again," he instructed me, taking my hand in both of his own. "It is watched. I deflected police attention from you by telling them that you were there gathering information for me. You have escaped the raid by the skin of your teeth. I have been waiting here, pacing, all evening, waiting for you—or for news of your arrest."

"My God, Homes!" I cried.

"Promise me," he said earnestly. "Promise me you will not return."

"I promise," I said, my hand still clasped in his. Then I realised the implications. My last scrap of earthly comfort, closeness, satisfaction, was now gone. I put my head in my hands. I despaired, amongst the wine glasses and the remains of our feast.

He rose and rested his hand on my shoulder.

"I know what you are feeling, where will you go for a human embrace, to ease your loneliness and grief? When will you next receive a loving kiss?"

"Yes," I groaned, all pretence set aside.

"Now," he said, and promptly kissed me. A sweet kiss. His lips were soft and wet with wine. "Will I not do as an adequate substitute for the whores of the Military Club?"

"Holmes!" I whispered.

He looked away from me, candlelight on his sharp profile, his hand still on my shoulder.

"I am no longer young, but I am healthy and clean. I was never beautiful. We have been friends for a very long time. Might you accept me as a substitute? I would not have my best friend walk unarmed into a den of lions—or, rather, a pit of scorpions."

"No," I said gently, patting the hand. His kiss tingled on my lips.

"No?" he asked, with a return to his cold, remorseless manner.

"Not as a substitute," I told him, taking the hand and kissing the palm. "You are no whore. Only as a lover could I accept you. If this is what you want, my dearest Holmes."

"It is," he averred.

"Why did you not ask me before?" I was curious, aroused, and afraid. Would this new turn of events destroy our ancient friendship, which had lasted so long and borne so much?

"I didn't *know* you were an invert," he said crossly, looking at me again. "I suspected as much, I gravely suspected as much, I hoped as much, but then you married, Watson. Before I could make up my mind to declare myself to you. It is a huge risk, you know. You might have turned away from me in disgust."

"Holmes, I would never..." I began. He interrupted me.

"You might have," he snapped.

"I might," I conceded. I kissed his hand again. "Are you, like me..."

"An invert? Of course. Consider the facts. I have never had even so much as a friendship with a woman except Mrs Hudson. All my close relationships are...well, with you."

"You have had lovers?" I asked, dazed. He might have been dallying with a whole brigade of guardsmen, as far as I would have known. I have never seen him look at a man with lust, never seen him dishevelled or red-mouthed with kissing, never even scented sex on him.

He sat down next to me on the sofa.

"When I was young. There was Sebastian, at least, we kissed and toyed and fancied ourselves in love. Then I smashed his world and he went to America and I decided that I had done with love."

"And you hadn't?" I smiled. He smiled, too, his rare and beautiful smile.

"Then a sturdy, strong, ex-army doctor limped into my life, and I found that I had not done with love after all."

I nearly choked on my Margaux.

"You've been in love with me all this time?" I cried. He patted me on the back.

"Let's have a glass of that Armagnac the Duc sent and consider the matter, since you have not run screaming from 221B in horror and loathing."

"My dearest Holmes," I whispered. I leaned into the hand cupping my cheek. "I am delighted, astonished, amazed. I have to tell you that I have loved you from the moment I saw you, I have always wanted you. I never knew you even thought of love."

"You knew how much I relied on you, trusted you, confided in you, cared for you," he said quietly.

"Yes," I said. I accepted the small glass of cognac. I was what Mrs Hudson called 'in a state'. "I knew. I saw it in your eyes."

"And you knew I had no other friend but you?"

"I never saw you with any confidential friend, male or female," I agreed.

"And you never will. Are you familiar with the myth that the Gods made men two-natured, then found their creations to be too strong?"

"Split them in half, so they spent their lives looking for their other halves, and didn't try to challenge the Gods again?" I remembered the story.

"I have been aware from the first time I spoke to you that you are my other half," he said.

"Oh," I said, struck by a revelation. "I am very dull. And of course you are mine."

"Bravo," he murmured, as he does when I make some halfway-decent piece of deduction. Being in love would not change Holmes because, by his account, he had always—Heavens!—been in love with me. All that time, while I had been finding other lovers and despairing of ever engaging his regard.

That called for more Armagnac-flavoured kisses. His lips were tentative. Whatever he had done with his friend Sebastian it had been a long time ago. But I had—God save me—experience enough for twenty. I would seduce him gently into making love, so that he would feel loved and cherished—and mine.

The thought was almost as intoxicating as the cognac.

He broke off the kiss, which was getting a little heated. I was aroused: he was, also.

"Rules," he announced. "This is a perilous enterprise, Watson, my dear Watson. Outside this flat we must be just what we have been. Agreed?"

"Of course," I said.

"Inside we must lock all the doors, be sure that if inspected, raided, we have two adequately slept-in beds—that is what condemned Lucius Paul. And no signs otherwise that two men have had a criminal connection. To that end I have caused fine linen towels to be bought. We can burn them at a pinch. And no love letters, no public kisses, nothing before an audience, even Mrs Hudson. We are risking a great deal, my dear."

"I know. I'll risk it if you will. We have enemies, Holmes, who would love to ruin us."

"I have enemies, you mean," he corrected me in his usual manner. Then he said wistfully, "Is love so good, that it is worth such peril? That you would go to that place in search of it?"

"I went here to slake my lusts with paid companions, which is not the same thing. That is not love. It is a transaction. And, yes, love is worth it and so I shall convince you. I agree to all your conditions."

"There is one more," he said, staring straight into my eyes.

"And that is?"

"That I am your only lover. I will not share you, Watson. If you are mine, you are mine alone."

"And you," I responded, chuckling, "Are mine. If I show you love and you acquire a taste for it, you may not then find a prettier man than a crippled doctor to share your bed."

He looked almost ill as he promised, hand upraised, that I would be the only one. Forever.

"I never thought you crippled," he told me. "I have always thought you most attractive. You have shoulders that Phidias might have carved, an admirable torso. And beautiful eyes."

"How long have you been preparing for this day?" I asked.

"I laid the towels in storage after the first month," he confessed.

"It is so sad, Holmes that we never spoke, that I never spoke, and you have spent all this time alone."

"I had you with me, and when you were gone, the memory of you," he told me. "It is late. Shall we retire?"

He held out his arm to me. I took it, and he led me to his bedroom. There, he paused. He had not taken Sebastian to bed, then. I shucked my slippers, took off my socks and trousers and underlinen, retaining my shirt and my dressing gown. Then I sat my lover down and unwrapped him as though he was a long desired gift, the very best of Christmas presents.

He did not flinch away from my touch, but I went slowly, allowing him time to object or draw back. I was effectively seducing a virgin, and I did not want to affront his modesty. He stripped pliably, moving so that I could remove various articles. I peeled his dressing gown away, and then his shirt. Finally I could kiss his shoulder, his skin. He was wiry and muscular, pale and smooth. I tongued a nipple and heard him make a sharp gasp, as he did when he had solved some arcane problem. I shed the remains of my own clothes, slowly. If he had indeed been waiting for this sight as long as I had, I wanted him to enjoy it.

I am not much to look at. I am flabby round the middle, stocky, scarred, especially my right thigh where they had dug as many fragments of that damnable jezail bullet out of me as they could find, leaving enough to lame me for life. His eagle eyes examined me with cool, deep intelligence. He reached out and touched my chest, sliding his hand down until he paused on a round scar on my hip.

"Bullet?" he asked.

"Yes, I had forgotten about it. Lie down with me, on your pristine linens," I said.

"Such is courage," he murmured, and lay down naked in my naked embrace, his head on my shoulder, our legs intertwined, and I know there were angels singing, because I heard them.

We had to do surprisingly little wriggling to lie easy. We fitted together, knee and hip and arm and chest, and we kissed luxuriously. We had the whole night. We had the rest of our lives.

We started to move together, soon enough. Heat grew between us. I found his sex and it leapt gratefully into my hand. He found mine, and I put both our hands and our cocks together, to slide together, thigh and chest, heat rising, mouths open and biting, kisses which grew wilder and wilder. I heard him panting, or was it me?

'Petit mort', they call it. Little death. If I had died then as my lover reached it with me, I would have died blessed.

I mopped us clean with his fine linen and folded him back into my arms.

"So strange," he murmured into my ear. "My dearest Watson, my...my love. It was not like that with..." he fell silent, perhaps not liking to name his previous lover while he was in bed in my company, though I did not mind.

"You were very young," I told him. "Making love is a skill like any other. Are you pleased, my dearest Holmes?"

"More than I thought possible," he said. "I see that you have much to teach me."

"It will be my pleasure," I assured him with perfect verity. No truer statement has ever been made.

He leaned up on one elbow and looked into my face, worried.

"Your pardon, dearest Watson, did my small effort please you? It felt so natural, so easy..."

"Two halves of the same whole, remember? Either knows what will please the other. I have never been so pleased, my love, my love."

I kissed him again. He kissed me back. Then he broke the kiss. This was beginning to be a bad habit of his.

"Sussex," he said flatly. "I do not insist on the location, but it must have a good connection to a town line."

"Holmes?" I asked, utterly confused.

"If we survive, when we retire," he explained patiently, "I would like to go to a remote cottage in Sussex and keep bees. Will you come with me?"

I laughed. He had mapped out the rest of our lives, after only one encounter.

"Sussex, yes, I like Sussex, and I have no objection to bees as long as they are your bees. We shall have a small cottage and a woman to come in by the day, and honey for tea."

"That's settled, then," he said. He buried his long nose in my neck, tightened his arms around me, and fell asleep.

So did I. I slept deep. I rose in time to unlock the apartment doors, wallow like a hippopotamus in my own bed to convincingly unmake it, and return to Holmes. I locked his bedroom door then, before Mrs H came and brought breakfast, I woke him with sleepy kisses and made use of his fine linen towels again.

I have never been so happy. I needed to write an account of it, to make it real to me, though no one will ever read it until we are long dead. And I hope that we have our Sussex cottage. I'm sure that Holmes will do very well with his hives, and I am very fond of honey.

Dr John Watson, MD

Becoming
By Morgan Black

Winter

"This is Bea," John says, careful, uncertain.

Not a client then.

Sherlock stills, bites his tongue. He turns towards the window and plucks a discord on his violin, frowning at the London rain.

Sherlock knows how to sting. His deductions would be scathing.

John is waiting for the barb.

Say something.

A draft huffs through the flat. Voices on the stairs. "Is he always like that?'

The door slams.

Alone again.

Spring

There's blood on his forehead because the lintel was too low and Sherlock too tall: too busy being busy to mind his own skin, and because he likes it when John fusses and tends him.

Smiling.

No Bea buzzing around John now. Just the two of us in the great hive of London.

Summer

3am

Too hot to sleep, John pads downstairs where Sherlock has lingered, experimenting, *avoiding,* this thing which has grown between them.

John stops still.

Sherlock is by the window stealing the breeze, pale skin bare, honey-gold beneath the streetlamps. John has never wanted anything so desperately.

Sherlock's gaze settles over him.

"John," he whispers.

No sweeter nectar ever beckoned.

Autumn

Curled around him, deep inside him, back to belly in their bed, their slow-fast rhythm gathering pleasure with touch and tongue. Symbiotic. Nectar and bee. *Sherlock and John.*

This is what they have become.

These Things Understood
By Poppy Alexander

"John! I need your help!"

It's a mild demand, more "I've got him on the ground, but you've got the handcuffs," than "someone unexpectedly has a knife and it isn't me," so John does not run—nor even jog—to where Sherlock is crouched behind a rose-bush hedge, though his stride is sufficiently purposeful that a uniformed copper stands aside without John begging pardon as he passes.

"*John!*"

"I'm here. Sherlock. I'm right here. What is it?"

One knee is on a mostly-dry flagstone tile surrounded though it is by damp, spongy moss, and Sherlock's head is bowed, body bent halfway between looking closely at—what? nothing John can see—*something* there on the garden floor, and rising to resume his feet. His elbow is propped on his upright knee; his palm turns up and he summons John closer with rolling fingers.

"There's a bee. In my hair, there's a bee."

John tilts his head.

"Sorry?"

"I don't want to ruin its day, but I also don't particularly want it on my head, and it's been wandering around up there long enough I think it may be lost."

Sherlock's hair is well overdue for a trim; unruly at the best of times, the over-long, dark waves are positively voluptuous in their exuberance, barely controlled even with generous applications of gels, foams, and serums—not to mention a not-insignificant amount of coaxing with fingertips, cooed encouragements, and whispery pleas to *behave*.

"So, I should…" John begins, and sets his mouth taut to repress a rather wider grin than is likely appropriate at the scene of a daylight kidnapping.

"Free it, obviously." Sherlock's tone is drifting toward urgent, but his lowered voice and unnerving stillness are uncommon habits; John cannot recall the last time he observed them.

"Ah." John steps close by Sherlock's shoulder, leaning down to get a look between and among the thick waves that crown him. In the bright sunlight of early afternoon, his bordering-on-ebony hair reveals its startlingly numerous shades of dark-and-mysterious: cinnamon stick, elm tree bark, bitter chocolate, and John's favourite (for the sheer delightful surprise of it), coppery dark auburn. Sure enough, after a moment's inspection, there is a telltale rippling and bending, just a few inches back from the hairline above his forehead. John ventures the tip of one finger, gently rearranging.

"Do you see it?"

"Not exactly. Be still." Sherlock is still as a statue and has been since John rounded the corner, but now he is also quiet, and that is something worth noting, so John notes it.

There is a flicker of golden-yellow fuzz then, framed in the perfect circle of a single curl. John has a mild urge to pinch and stretch it, listening for the springing sound as it coils back toward Sherlock's scalp.

Instead, he comments, "Big fella."

"Yes, it's a bumblebee," Sherlock says, and John would have expected him to sound impatient but instead he sounds subdued.

"All right then, let's see if we can't—" John doesn't finish, bites his bottom lip in his concentration, and with fingers and thumbs of both hands, gently pinches carefully-selected locks and draws them up and aside so that more of the bee is revealed. Its wings are low and still; it marches northeast. John extends one middle finger to hook another few strands and drag them aside. He can see the hairs slip through the fuzz of the bee's thorax, and this seems to remind it that a detective's head is no place for it, and it rises rather like a helicopter, nearly vertical, then flies drunkenly off in the opposite direction of the nearby rose hedge.

"Godspeed, friend," John says jovially, but slender hanks of Sherlock's hair are still wound around his fingertips, held tight between knuckles and thumb pads, and Sherlock remains silent and still. John tests his hypothesis: he tugs, firm and steady, and given close proximity to the crown of Sherlock's bent head, he sees the scalp strain as he holds the locks taut.

Sherlock hums a quiet sigh.

John releases him, straightens up, takes a half-step back. "There you are, entirely bee-free," he says in his most overtly jocular tone. Sherlock lifts his face to meet John's gaze and a wordless agreement settles between them—one of hundreds, if not thousands, they have shared over their years together—that, once confirmed, is immediately dismissed. The change in Sherlock as he gets back to work reminds John of a pinball machine: the silent, silver ball is flung forward and all at once: lights, bells, flippers, music, and—if one isn't careful— a tilt. Sherlock's brain winds up to speed in a matter of seconds, potential energy converted to kinetic just like that. As Sherlock bends low to sniff at the ground, John passes time admiring a few more of the fat, golden bees pendulum-swinging from blossom to blossom on the hedge.

*

Who knows how these things come to be understood? Lovers avidly learning each other. The silent understanding that *this* is how we fit each other. Puzzling bodies into place, yours there, mine here, more this, less that. Velocity. Pressure. Tempo. Volume. May I? Of course. Did you? Not really. Well then what about? Might do; let's try that next time. Why not now? Why not indeed? An interior catalogue of ticklish twitches and languid stretches, back-of-mind notes taken in response to a secret, shared vocabulary of sighs and moans and—*oh, yes!*—shouts.

And so now that they are on the descending side of the learning curve, John no longer remembers how it came to be that they can pass a three-second glance back and forth between them—even in public view— and both fully appreciate its weight and shape without a word. *Will you—for me—please? Of course—for you— always.* Perhaps once upon a time it was an exceptionally delicious whine in response to a tentatively aggressive touch, which invited an experimental test of a perceived boundary, which elicited a fervent kiss or a locking of legs about rolling hips or a *more...more...dear god more...*Surely it was evolutionary, and the most explicit discussions amount to but a few murmured sentences in the safety of post-ecstatic exhaustion, cloaked in darkness, whispered against pillows.

I'm afraid—
I'm not.
You'll stop me if—
I will...but I likely won't.
I know, but promise anyway, will you?
I do. I promise...Now...do it again.

54

It is just the way they fit each other. Meaningful glances, bodies angled toward or away, tacit acknowledgements…and very few words. Which is not to say they do not talk. As now:

"Come over here and let me pet you."

Often it begins with a gentle *hey, c'mere*, or a dirty smirk over some sexual pun oozing out of the telly they are barely half-watching, or one simply asking the other if he is coming to bed. This evening, they slip off jackets and loosen cuff-buttons, plug mobile phones into chargers, pull a stack of takeaway menus from a kitchen drawer for later, not talking much, for there is no need. The solution to the case was not, as it happened, between the flagstones at which Sherlock stared as John freed the captive bee, but rather in some ephemeral combination of internet searching for Portuguese weather reports; coincidental (or not) dates of long-ago crimes which Sherlock found stored on his own, cranium-encased hard drive; and the strange use of possessive pronouns in a witness statement. They'd clocked out at precisely five o'clock, upstanding workingmen both, neither yet hungry for dinner. This evening, it begins with John, in his usual kitchen chair facing the worktops, pulled away at an angle so that he is one-third at table and two-thirds merely near it.

"Come on, then."

It is more request than command; John wants to. He enjoys smoothing Sherlock's angles with his hands, which too often seem useless now they're no longer fit for service to queen and country.

Sherlock, prowling the lounge with no obvious destination, stalks in a slow U-bend to aim himself toward John—a silent, immediate response to having been summoned. When he reaches the table, he pulls out the chair diagonal to John's and cradles his head on his folded arms, spends a moment adjusting the way his forehead nestles there inside his elbow. Eventually, he flings one forearm out in front and rolls his neck a bit, at last settling.

John leans forward and stretches to scratch what he can reach of Sherlock's bent back, which isn't much, the top half of the top half of the near side. Sherlock inhales hard, but when he exhales, it is stretched and deliberate, and he softens, sliding the chair back a few inches, his upper body elongating as he releases tension.

John draws the back of Sherlock's shirt collar down just enough, making space to kiss the back of his neck, mostly chaste, *hello you, it's me, fancy meeting you here*, and this melts Sherlock further. John sits back, and singles out one pronounced, dark wave to pinch between thumb and forefinger, gently gliding along its curve. Then another, this time stretching it out and back, out and back, just fiddling. Sherlock's breathing grows shallow and the passage of air through his lungs raises and lowers his still-rounded back. John wriggles three fingertips to bury them against his scalp, and rakes across the back of his head, low, behind his ears. He swirls the middle finger to wind up a curl at Sherlock's nape, then releases it as he drags his hand back.

Sherlock doesn't like to be touched much. He does not hold hands because to surrender even one makes him feel handcuffed—he needs to type, to swipe, to flip pages, fold corners, smooth the front placket of his shirt—and although he did make a try at it—for a bit—at first—it was quickly apparent it was too much to ask of him.

John touches Sherlock's wrist sometimes—across the dinner table, or as they walk—and it's enough to have communicated the urge; he does not require or even request consummation. Sherlock will tolerate brief kisses dropped in his hair or on his shoulder as John passes; nearly every one of these is given while Sherlock is so engrossed in what he is reading or studying or thinking that it would matter not a jot if John flicked his ear instead of kissing his cheek, but John likes to make the gesture nonetheless.

Embracing, hugging, holding each other…all tolerable if the context is (a) reunion after time apart exceeding eight hours; (b) affirmation that one or both has not prematurely, violently expired due to recent foul play or negligence; or (c) clearly sexual or at least very likely heading down that track. Once the scent of mutual desire reaches the air, Sherlock allows—invites, welcomes, sometimes demands—any and every touch John wishes to give. There is some membrane he must pass through, it seems, from the everyday world— where thought and reason are so all-consuming that being touched is an annoying, overstimulating distraction—into some otherworld (whether it is of dreams, or reserved for pleasure, or merely unguarded, Sherlock has never articulated—though John tends to think of this rarified space as *Body and Soul*, while the rest of Sherlock's existence is singularly *Mind*). Once Sherlock has agreed or decided or been coaxed across that ribbon-edged border, every unadorned acre of him is on offer, from the sole of his exquisite foot to the soft, bite-inviting skin of his belly to the lovely, mad, usually-too-long hair on his head.

Minutes have passed and Sherlock is as soft as he gets without being asleep. John is scrubbing gently (*so* gently…Sherlock is tenderheaded in the extreme, hence the procrastinated haircuts), swirling spirals all over the back and crown of Sherlock's head. His curls react against the interference by breaking apart and expanding like a frightened cat trying to look bigger. Sherlock hums long and low, pure contentment, and so John digs deeper, drags his fingertips with more precision, the edges of his fingernails lightly scratching. The fingers on Sherlock's stretched-out arm, which have been resting loosely curled on the tabletop, suddenly clutch at it as if he, too, can dig in. John goes on scratching in widening circles that travel the entire surface of Sherlock's scalp from the back of his neck all the way to his forehead, out to the temples, then back again and around and around. Sherlock voices another noise, no longer purring, but gasping, somewhere between protest and pleasure.

"Had enough?" John asks then, quietly, rolling a thick hank of Sherlock's hair between thumb and forefinger, winding it around his fingertip.

Sherlock hum-grunts in the negative.

"I won't ask again."

Sherlock nods against the inside of his elbow, affirming his understanding.

It's a fickle thing; sometimes despite Sherlock's desire for it, John's hands in his hair make him squirmy and irritable, his scalp too tender, feeling his space is being invaded. At other times, John can't scratch too deep, can't yank too suddenly, can't pull too hard— Sherlock will gasp and grab tight to John's wrists, whining for more…more…*more*. One thing John has come to learn over time is that if it's not right, Sherlock will know from the start. He won't ask again if Sherlock's enjoying it, if it's too much, if John should stop, because Sherlock doesn't need him to ask again. If it's too much, it's too much from the very first minute.

So John rakes his fingers in lazy figure-eights for a few seconds more, and Sherlock himself seems a bit lazy in response to the stimulus, sighing and soft-limbed, face down in the crook of his arm on the kitchen tabletop. John bunches his fingers into a fist, catching as much as he can of the hair at Sherlock's crown, and drags Sherlock along behind him as he springs up and strides toward the bedroom. Long, pale arms in their turned-back shirt cuffs flail, and long, pale hands grabbing at John's hand and wrist—not to free himself, only to give himself leverage as he scrambles to follow, kicking his chair away behind him, making its feet scrape the floor, and bashing his thigh against the corner of the table. John's pull is steadily medium-hard, but now and then he pulses his wrist, making Sherlock jump forward.

Bent double, clinging to John's forearm, Sherlock whimpers at the new sensation, his mouth staying open as his breath comes harder, from the shock of pain and from arousal. Once they're in the bedroom, John draws him up hard, practically throws him where he wants him to go. Sherlock's momentum carries him toward the bed, where he catches himself on its edge with both hands.

"Here," John demands. Not shouting, certainly, but firm. He points to the floor in front of him, and Sherlock kneels there with his knees touching the toes of John's shoes, bowing his head, offering his ridiculous, sumptuous curls. All ten of John's delicate fingers sink in, and comb back and back in overlapping, alternating strokes, from the crown all the way down the back of his head to the nape of his neck. Sherlock's shoulders shudder and collapse; he lets go a low moan.

It's not about power play, domination and submission, the elaborate rules people create for themselves which Sherlock and John find too self-consciously artificial, like playacting in ill-fitting suits. In their do-as-we-like comfort zone, it's not about one kneeling and one giving orders; it's about one needing and one giving solace. It is only what it is: a thing they do, one among many. If pressed on the issue, John might admit not minding the permission to take charge of Sherlock a bit—and not only in the way that has him reminding Sherlock to put on shoes when a client is coming. And in response to John's firmer hand and sterner tone of voice, Sherlock becomes unusually pliable, seems to relish the chance to surrender, though if pressed on that issue, Sherlock would likely deny it.

John twists two fingers in, just above Sherlock's right ear, curls them to secure his grip, and bends at the waist as he pulls *down*. Sherlock's head, then neck and shoulder, and finally his torso fold sideways in a ripple, inevitably following. Just when it seems he must let go or Sherlock overbalance and collapse, John reverses course and drags him upright again. Once his head is centered atop his neck, John loosens his grip, tightens it, and gives Sherlock a good shake, which elicits a high-pitched grunt, and inspires Sherlock to reach for John's wrist again. It's reflexive; it doesn't mean *stop*.

Neither is it about pain. The unpredictable, intense *sensation* is what Sherlock is after: bursting, burning, steady throbbing and sharp pricking, unbalanced, off-kilter. John has come to realise (though Sherlock has never said), that John's fingers in his hair—fists tangling, knuckles digging, nails scraping, the yank, tug, and pull at his oh-so-sensitive scalp—serve as a reminder that Sherlock's head is for more than just thinking. His head houses his very big brain, of course, but it is also attached to his body; Sherlock seems more aware than he used to, *before*, of his body's capabilities—that it can die of pleasure, safe here within the walls of the rooms they share—and of its fragility— that it can die, too, of violence out there in the world. Sherlock no longer pretends he is immune or oblivious to danger; he still never hesitates to run toward it, but in calculating his route, now weighs up relative risks in a way he never did, *before*. John reckons, with a strange, swollen heat rising in his chest and throat, that just as he has found a reason to keep himself breathing well into next week, Sherlock has more reason now, to keep out of harm's way. There's no need to speak of it, and so they never do.

Sherlock bites his bottom lip and lets out a high whine as John rolls his head in circles on his sturdy neck by a fistful of hair just above his forehead, where it is longest and easy to grip. His eyes are closed, his lashes damp, the skin of his throat beneath his open collar flushing pink. John's own breath comes quicker now, because the flush and the damp closed eyes remind him of other times, touching Sherlock in altogether other ways, and his focus momentarily shifts from Sherlock's need to his own, which is persistent, aching, rampant.

"How is it?" he mutters. Rhetorical. He can see it's exactly what's required. "Hurts, does it? Hurts this pretty, sweet head of yours?"

Sherlock is sat back on his heels, and John draws him up and forward until he is standing on his knees. Wrapping his free hand around the back of Sherlock's skull, cradling, then digging in, scraping up a handful of the thick curls at the nape, John shoves him close.

Sherlock's mouth comes open obediently and he roars a hot exhalation against the front placket of John's trousers. His long-fingered hands rest soft against John's thigh and rump. John releases his grip in favour of trailing all ten fingertips against Sherlock's scalp in slow, scrolling meanders. Sherlock hums against him and John thinks he might die of it, then the deft hands move to John's button and zip.

He tilts his face upward, following the suggestion of John's persuasive petting and genteel tugs at pinched-off, slender locks. Sherlock's eyes are wide open, and his smile is soft and crooked with bliss. John longs to kiss him, but he will save it. Instead, he works his way across the back of Sherlock's head by fingerfuls, pinch and pull, pinch and pull, pinch and pull, in steady rhythm. Sherlock groans, low and loud, and John feels it in the base of his spine.

John's trousers are opened and shimmied down his legs, then Sherlock's cool hands come to rest at the sides of John's bare thighs, fingers sliding lightly, absently, up and down, smoothing and disturbing the hair there even as John works to piece apart single strands at the back of Sherlock's bent head, pulsing shivers of multiple tiny tugs against each one, like the pricking of a pin in reverse. Sherlock is nuzzling his nose and chin and open, dry lips against John's heavy prick, nosing into his pubic hair, tickling against his bollocks, and all the while his hands slip gently up and down the backs of John's thighs. John continues quick-pulling those single strands of Sherlock's hair, and a noise emanates from behind Sherlock's nose—a soft whimper—that threatens to break John's heart. Changing course, he winds up his forefinger in one thick hank of hair and pulls up and out with firm, relentless pressure. He can feel Sherlock pulling against him to avoid bending his neck; the tension is exquisite. Sherlock's tongue flicks out to tease his own lips and the side of John's cock as nimble fingers work the buttons of his own shirt to reveal his rosy-mottled chest and nipples hard as pebbles. Sherlock shrugs, tugs, and the shirt sails to the floor: monogrammed, million-thread count litter.

John's hands dig into the hair at Sherlock's crown and nape and pull him—not his hair, not only his hair, pulling *him*, pulling him close because John needs him *now*—selfishly, urgently closer. Sherlock makes a delicious low hum of eager assent—*ah-mmm*—and lets himself be pulled, open-mouthed, forward, tight-lipped, back, forward, wet, licking, back, pulling, pulling, *pulling*, fingers dug in and wound round and round, rolls his tongue anti-clockwise, lets himself be pulled, opens his throat, swallows, humming, pulling close, pulling back, pulling tight, pulling hard, lets himself, lets himself, lets himself be pulled.

At last, John releases him just long enough for them to quickly finish undressing (leaning together for dirty-tasting kisses, muttering non-sentences: *so good...want you...gorgeous...come on then*) and relocate to the bed, still rumpled and stale from when they last left it. Sherlock arranges pillows so John can rest his upright back against them, straddles John's thighs, his shoulders and throat just there asking to be bitten, and so John bites, just there asking to be kissed and licked, and so John kisses and licks. Sherlock settles and resettles, leans his long torso forward until John's mouth finds the curve where neck meets shoulder. Sherlock licks his long fingers, his pale palm, wraps the other hand around John's bicep to steady them. His thighs tighten around

John's hips as he finds the angle, encircles them both, and he begins a desperate, languid roll.

Sherlock makes that sound again, that whimper, stirring the hair behind John's ear with needy breath. John reaches both hands, one clutching Sherlock's hip, one worming fingers into his hair: ruined, wrecked, mad as if John has already had him, wrong in a way that makes John lick his lips when he sees what he has wrought-by-invitation upon that otherwise tender, untouchable head. He traces fingertip-curlicues against Sherlock's scalp, earning a delicious moan and a jump and shudder of his hips as his long, pale hand works in counterpoint motion to his long, pink prick sliding hard against John's own cock, slick with saliva, the sticky desire that oozes between them, imperfect, inelegant, hot. Rough. Hot.

"More," Sherlock murmurs, and the tip of his tongue as it traces the upper edge of John's ear is half-dry from panting. John obeys, gives him more, a quick yank here, then here, then here, now tangling up and pulling steadily down, until Sherlock voices protest that isn't really protest at all.

Sherlock's hand slips, or he moves it, leaves John bereft of his touch even as he goes on stroking himself, low, moaning, *Oh*s escaping on each jagged breath. John shifts his grip, tugs hard at a small lock near the nape of Sherlock's neck.

"Mind your manners, Holmes." Sherlock quick-licks his palm again, rushing to comply. John sucks air as Sherlock stills his rocking pelvis, brings his entire focus to working them both within the circle of his fingers. John lets go the bony hip to cover Sherlock's hand with his own, gathers a handful of overlong hair at his crown and pulls hard and long, bending Sherlock's neck, baring his throat, making him groan. "Pretty picture," John mutters. "This neck of yours. The curve of it." He pulls harder, more. "When I'm pulling your hair."

"Yes."

"Pulling hard."

"Yes."

"Hurts."

"*Ah...yes...*"

John's hand around Sherlock's hand grips tighter, guiding his pace. Sherlock whines; John pulls. Sherlock shudders, hiccups a gasp, and John (*pulling*) opens his eyes wide to take in the pretty picture of Sherlock here close in front of him: chin and jaw held high, neck straining, smooth and taut, chest flushed pink, belly quivering, long fingers between John's fingers and—*oh Christ*—spurting, moaning, stroking, dripping, a shiver, letting John guide him, *fuck that's beautiful*, and when John finally lets go of his hair his head collapses forward only far enough to see, muttering, *for me now, oh John please, I want you to, I want to see you, for me, for me...*

John draws Sherlock's face close, wants to kiss the swollen lips, finds he can't because he's shouting. They brush bristly jaws together, John bites, not hard, no marks, *oh yes, yes John, please for me, all for me.*

Once their breath is caught and they are minimally tidied, they fold themselves into a new shape, Sherlock's miles-long arms and legs wound round and round, his head there low on John's chest so John can gently—*so* gently—draw his fingers over the entire landscape of Sherlock's tender scalp, checking for injury, certainly, but calming, soothing, walking the two of them back out into the world on the pads of his roving fingers. Soon they'll rise, and one will phone for a takeaway while the other runs the water to warm it, and then they'll share the shower, talk about the case or about prospects for the next one or about nothing, dress in clothes soft enough for sleep, eat spicy food and toast each other with mugs of milky tea, and their bare feet will find each other in the space between their two chairs. Who knows how these things come to be understood? The puzzle of bodies, of habits, lives; two people discovering the ways they fit each other.

The One Good Thing To Come Out Of War
By Brittany Russ

There are two sounds that are unmistakable in the dead of night: the metallic ping of someone carelessly dropping a pin to the ground, and the severely hushed tones of two lovers endeavouring to be silent. The latter was true of an abandoned barn, deep in Nazi-occupied France, though these lovers had more reasons than most not to get caught.

John Watson was a captain of the British army, and looked quite like anyone would expect a Captain of His Majesty's to look: strong, well presented, with an immaculately trimmed moustache. A firm believer that even in a war, a gentleman must find time for a cup of tea and a shave.

Sherlock Holmes, on the other hand, was an eccentric but brilliant SOE agent. He and his team of Baker Street Irregulars had three munitions factory sabotages and a main supply train derailment under their belts within the last two weeks. Holmes could make a cup of coffee last all day by sporadically forgetting and remembering he had made one, and he had yet to completely wash the soot from the last successful explosion out of his hair.

Chalk and cheese, really, but Watson believed their love was all the stronger for it. Shame they happened to meet in the middle of a war. It was a damn nuisance for restricting their time together.

"One day I will see more of you than the small of your back," Watson sighed, running his hand over the bare strip of Holmes' skin exposed to him.

On his knees and elbows before him Holmes squirmed a little under the touch. "And on that day perhaps I will see your face instead of this ridiculous radio," Holmes replied. He had finished connecting the two portions of his B2 radio and was currently setting the frequencies to contact London. "But do try not to talk, my dear Watson, you do tend to lose focus." Holmes wiggled his arse against the heat of Watson's crotch to make a point.

Watson scoffed. "I should be insulted you can concentrate at all," he said, taking the hint and continuing his steady thrusts.

"Don't be," Holmes assured him. "There's a war on, one must learn to multitask." He pulled out his French copy of *The ABC of Bee Culture* which was both his code book and a part of his SOE disguise as a peasant beekeeper. He readied the headset and glanced at his watch. "Thirty seconds left, my dear Watson."

Two minutes before and one minute after transmission was at most all the time they could risk. It was enough to get them riled, but rarely enough to satisfy. The sexual frustration built each time, but the only other choice was to abstain completely. They had both agreed that was hardly an option. The times were too uncertain not to take every opportunity they were given. What if the war stretched on for years? What if one of them was killed? What if, even after everything Holmes had done for the SOE, they still charged him with homosexuality? His usefulness in the war effort was the only thing keeping him safe, and who knew how that would change once the need for espionage ceased to matter.

No, Watson would take what little of Holmes he could get. He pushed up Holmes' shirt as far as he could and began a quicker thrust. It still wasn't the part of his lover he wished to see the most but it was more than he saw on an average night.

Watson had never been a quiet lover. He believed passion was the most honest thing you could show, and it burned him deeply Holmes didn't know that side of him. *Another reason to survive the war,* Watson thought, because if anyone deserved to see the passion that lay within Watson, it was Holmes.

For now, however, Watson clenched his jaw and concentrated more than he would like to on his breathing. Each moan or call of his lover's name he had to choke back, he gave a stroke to Holmes' cock instead. It didn't take long before his hand caught up with his thrusts.

Holmes caught his knuckle between his teeth and bit down hard enough to leave indents. He was finding it far more difficult than usual to concentrate. Watson clearly needed this, and Holmes was beginning to realise so did he. But thirty seconds was slipping by far too quickly, and Holmes began to think he may have to do something drastic.

A few more seconds, Watson thought. A few more seconds and perhaps they could reach satisfaction. Watson could feel it, months of frustration building up to finally be released. He could hear Holmes' heavy breathing intermingled with soft moans, feel the shudders running through his body. He had to be as close as Watson. Just a few more seconds…

"Stop," Holmes demanded, holding the headset closer to his ear as London began passing along their encoded message. Watson swore like a sailor under his breath but did as he was told. His whole body shook in frustration, but he would never jeopardise the war effort for the sake of a few more seconds with his lover.

He began to pull out, knowing the second the transmission was over they would need to pack up the radio and flee, but as he moved back, Holmes moved with him until he was seated firmly in Watson's lap, still listening intently to the Morse code coming through his head set.

"Holmes?" Watson's question was met with silence, but he knew better than to ask again, and at any rate he had no reason to complain. He lent his forehead on Holmes' shoulder and waited, doing his best to slow his breathing to a normal rate.

After two minutes of listening and a quick flip through his code book, Holmes lent forward and tapped out a short reply before throwing his headset down.

"Holmes?" Watson asked again, snapping his lover out of his daze over the transmission. "Should we not be on our way?"

Holmes was suddenly struck by how foolish his plan had been. "Quite right, yes." He unceremoniously dumped himself out of Watson's lap and turned to face him. "Sorry, terribly selfish of me, but I thought we might have time to finish what we started. But of course I wouldn't ask you to risk your life for a mere dalliance…"

Watson lent forward and halted Holmes' rambling with a solid kiss. He slid his hands up into Holmes' hair as Holmes pulled him down on top of him. "You're hardly a dalliance," Watson said, working Holmes' trouser all the way off.

"I will admit it was a poor choice of word." Holmes wrapped his legs around Watson's waist and let the lips of his good Captain swallow the moan that was elicited at the new-found angle this position offered.

Holmes busied his mouth with kissing Watson's neck to muffle any more unexpected moans, and Watson thrilled at being able to press his lips close to Holmes' ear and let him hear his whispered cries of passion.

Holmes was the first to fall, biting down on Watson's shoulder as he clawed at his back. Watson didn't last much longer, muffling his own cry into Holmes' neck.

Of all the things Watson noticed about Holmes in that moment, the one that stood out the most was that beneath all the dirt and grime that came from months without a decent bath, Holmes smelt faintly of honey. Watson smiled to himself. From now on, that scent would always remind him of Holmes.

For a long moment they didn't move. For Watson it took all his energy not to burst into tears. He had spent so much time terrified they would never share a moment like this that the relief was overwhelming.

"Stiff upper lip, old boy," Holmes said, his own emotion betrayed in the tone of his voice.

Watson snorted. "Quite right, old cock, hardly the time for blubbing." They pulled themselves together and began to redress.

"You may not hear from me for two weeks," Holmes said as he packed the radio back into its two separate containers. He handed one to Watson and patted him on the shoulder. "Do try not to get yourself shot again in the mean time."

"If I hadn't gotten shot in the first place, we wouldn't have met," Watson reminded him.

"Precisely, I don't want you running off and meeting someone else while I'm gone."

"Well, there's a thought." Watson smirked, before leaning in for one last kiss. "If there was one good thing to come out of this war, it was meeting you," he said, sincerely.

Holmes smiled. "My sentiments precisely." He gave him one last peck before they were off in opposite directions.

Two weeks was not an unusual amount of time for Holmes to disappear, though Watson would always worry throughout. At least now he had fresh memories to distract and his honey rations to make it feel like Holmes was close.

That Escalated Quickly
By Anarion

Lestrade woke to someone pulling on his arm. He opened one eye.

"Sherlock? How did you get in here? The door was locked!"

"In a manner of speaking."

"What?"

"Never mind." With that Sherlock Holmes dramatically threw himself into the armchair in the corner.

Silence.

Lestrade groaned. "Sherlock, what are you doing here? It's two in the morning."

"John is in Edinburgh."

"Yeah...?"

"I'm bored."

"Get out!"

Lestrade dropped back into bed and pulled the duvet over his head. He didn't even hear Sherlock leave.

*

Lestrade woke to something wet on his face.

He pulled the damp flannel off and regarded his visitor with a sigh.

"Sherlock, please tell me that you're not here again because you were bored..."

"John is..."

"...still in Edinburgh, I know."

"I need something to do!"

"Fine! There's a cold case file on the table. The mysterious death of an amateur beekeeper."

"Were you expecting me? I'm touched."

"Get out."

*

Lestrade woke up screaming, ice cold and wet to the skin. Next to his bed stood Sherlock, holding a bucket.

"Sherlock, goddammit! Have you lost your mind?"

"I solved the case."

"Of course you did. It couldn't wait until tomorrow?"

"The victim accidentally killed herself. Poison honey. Nothing you can do."

"THEN WHY ARE YOU HERE?"

"I just wanted to tell you that John is back."

Bees and Butterflies
By Tessa Barding

He is going through his daily warm-up routines when the butterfly finds its way into the sitting room of 221B Baker Street. Holmes frowns and for a fleeting moment wonders whether he should close the windows. It would certainly keep the neighbours' ghastly phonograph music out, along with butterflies, but it's lovely outside and he likes how the sunlight makes the dust particles glitter. When he empties his mind – the way he usually does when warming up on the violin – they cease being dust particles and become manifestations of the music he plays. Sparkling notes that dance through the sitting room, tiny twinkling stars.

He follows the flight of the insect – *pieris rapae* – with his eyes and adapts his playing to the irregular flutter of the pale, translucent wings. The butterfly disapproves of his interpretation of its flight and leaves through the second window.

He closes his eyes and starts improvising around Rachmaninoff's *Prelude*, the tension leaving his shoulders as he loses himself in the music.

It's been a rough three weeks. The last case has cost him sleep and a few pounds but it has earned him the satisfaction of having been right from the start. It has also earned him a few glares from Dr Watson.

Ah, Watson. He smiles when he hears a muffled curse coming from the doctor's room, changes from C-sharp minor to E major and launches into Bach's third partita for solo violin.

Things have changed since Watson has returned from the Somme. He's stealing glances when he thinks Holmes isn't looking, and Holmes is stealing glances back. Watson is a handsome man with thick chestnut hair and smiling hazel eyes, almost as tall as Holmes himself but not as lanky. Well, not lanky at all. Watson has a good pair of shoulders and strong arms and legs from the boxing lessons he used to take. He can no longer box or play tennis after very nearly losing his left leg to a grenade but he has begun putting himself through relentless physical exercises because not only does he loathe relying on the help of others, but because being physically active helps him cope with his changed reality. He never mentions either to Holmes but Holmes knows anyway. He hears the grunts and the occasional *thump* coming from Watson's room and he sees it in the shoulders that no longer slump like they did during the long, depressing months of convalescence. Besides, while the limp is still there it's no longer as pronounced and Watson has switched from the much hated crutches to a less obtrusive cane.

Holmes, who is so good at reading others and who excels at picking up the tiniest of detail, is uncertain about what to make of the stolen glances. Watson has always been a ladies' man, and Holmes? Well, he has never given the whole business much thought. There's always something more interesting to pursue, an intellectual puzzle to solve, a fascinating subject to look into. And yet… thinking of Watson has begun to make his body hum of late.

He pulls the bow across the strings for the final chord, lets it hover in the air and follows the last note with his inner ear.

"I've always liked that piece."

He turns around. Watson is leaning against the doorframe, smiling at him. His braces hang by his sides and he's in his socks.

"I know," Holmes replies and carefully puts bow and violin down. "That's why I played it."

"For me? Why?"

"Consider it an incentive."

Watson raises his eyebrows and Holmes shrugs.

"I heard you."

"Heard me?"

"Going through your gymnastics. I thought, perhaps, some music that you like might help." He feels silly when he says it and in an effort to conceal his unease, he makes for the kitchen. "Would you like some tea?"

"That would be lovely, thank you," Watson says and moves so that Holmes can pass him.

Their shoulders touch.

"Sorry," mumbles Watson and Holmes, at the same time, "Forgive me."

They stand rooted to the spot, caught in a moment of awkward silence. Watson's scent hits Holmes' senses and he inhales deeply. There are remnants of the medical soap he uses to scrub his arms and hands – he has started to work at a small private clinic, on an hourly basis –, there's the cologne he's splashed on this morning, there's a faint whiff of fresh sweat from his exercises, but most of all, there's Watson's unique scent, that of a clean, healthy male.

A single drop of sweat is running down the side of his neck. Holmes follows it with his eyes and, giving in to what must surely be temporary insanity mixed with a dash of idiotic recklessness, leans forward and licks it away.

"What are you doing, Holmes," Watson whispers. It doesn't really sound like a question and he doesn't flinch either, makes no effort to move out of the way.

Instead, he tilts his head to the side. It's barely noticeable and Holmes raises his eyes to Watson's face, searches for even the slightest hint of revulsion, for signs of imminent rejection. Watson's tongue darts out to wet his lips and his pupils are dilating when he feels Holmes' questioning look. There's his answer. *In for a penny –*

Watson's mouth is on his before he can finish the thought and they stand there, with their lips pressed together, and just as Holmes is beginning to think this is a horrible, embarrassing mistake, Watson parts his lips, teases Holmes' mouth open with his tongue that is warm and wet as it snakes past Holmes' teeth, but it's neither pushy nor intrusive. Watson is a good kisser, much more experienced than Holmes but Holmes is nothing if not ready to experiment. When he sucks on Watson's tongue, Watson's hands clamp around his upper arms and he moans.

Holmes breaks the kiss, concerned.

"Am I doing something wrong?" he asks, disliking how small his voice sounds.

"Wrong?" Watson cups Holmes' face with his hands and brings their foreheads together. "God, Holmes, the things I want to do to you." His thumbs sweep over Holmes' lips. "You have no idea how much I've wanted this. For so bloody long," he murmurs.

The truth of his statement is unmistakable; it presses against Holmes and it doesn't take particular observational skills to safely deduce that Watson is every bit as aroused as he is.

Truth is, there are plenty of things Holmes wants to do to Watson, too, although he cannot remember when it has first manifested, this idea, this craving – or even what has started it. The morning he walked in on

Watson in the bathroom, shaving, clad only in his pyjama trousers? He remembers admiring the pronounced V-shape of Watson's torso, terrified of being found staring yet unable to take his eyes off him. The moment he noticed Watson's lisp that only occurs when he's laughing and trying to speak at the same time? The way his right eyebrow quirks up when he's amused? The way he tips his fingers against his lips when he's thinking? It doesn't really matter now, does it? All that matters is that the doctor is kissing him again, and he's kissing him hard...

...and Holmes notices, absent-mindedly and with what little remains of his rationally working brain, that Watson is beginning to favour his right leg.

"Does your leg hurt?"

"My leg be damned," Watson says, irritated. "Yes, it does."

"Would you, ah," Holmes swallows, "would you like to sit down?"

The annoyance vanishes from Watson's face, is replaced by a mischievous grin. It's infectious and Holmes feels his own lips curve into a smile.

"You know what," Watson slowly says, as if in deep thought, "I think it would help if I lay down for a moment."

"Of course. Sofa or bed?" Holmes aims for a light tone but isn't sure if he's succeeding. His heartbeat has increased to an alarming rate and his palms are suddenly sweaty.

"Bed." Watson's voice leaves no doubt but the hand that's nestled against the small of Holmes' back clutches his shirt a little tighter. So he is nervous, too? *Interesting.*

They make it to Watson's room in an awkward shuffle, Watson's arm slung around Holmes' shoulder, Holmes holding on to Watson's waist, bodies pressed against each other at an odd angle, half sideways, half facing each other, and they stop when Watson's legs hit his bed. He lets himself fall backwards and Holmes lands on top of him, one of his elbows hitting Watson's solar plexus when he tries to steady himself.

"Ooof." It comes out as a grunt. "You're a lot heavier than you look."

"I'm sorry –" Holmes forgets what he's sorry for when Watson's legs open underneath him and he sinks in between them. One of Watson's hands travels down his back until it lands on his buttocks – his meagre buttocks, he thinks with a sudden stab of self-consciousness – and squeezes. Apparently he's not found all that lacking because Watson moans into the kiss and rubs himself against Holmes. When he pushes himself up into a sitting position, Holmes loses his balance and slides off the bed where he awkwardly lands on his knees.

For a moment, he's is afraid Watson will laugh at him but as he's at a loss about what to do next he stays where he is, aroused and confused, and waits for Watson's next move.

Watson does not laugh. He looks at him, cocks his head, narrows his eyes, then reaches up, grabs the back of his shirt and yanks it over his head in a swift move. He tosses it carelessly aside and throws Holmes a challenging look.

"Now you," he says. "Strip."

Holmes rises obediently, pushes his braces down and starts fumbling with the shirt buttons that seem too big and too small at the same time. It's like he's never unbuttoned a shirt before. He manages eventually, of course he does, pulls his undershirt over his head, too, and stands before Watson, half naked, feeling exposed and all too aware of his own slim and angular frame when he looks at the other man's broad shoulders and chest.

Watson's eyes travel along his upper body.

"Perfect," he murmurs and gives him an encouraging look. "Trousers, too."

Holmes swallows but there's something arousing about being ordered to strip and so he kneels down to unlace and remove his shoes, pulls his socks off, too, then straightens and opens the fly buttons with hands that are not quite steady. Watson is watching him with an intent look on his face, palming himself through his trousers. His unabashed interest takes some of Holmes' nervousness away and he relaxes, even begins enjoying himself. He opens the remaining buttons, hooks his thumbs into the waistbands of both his trousers and his underpants and raises his chin, waiting.

"Go on." It comes out as a hoarse whisper and Holmes pushes trousers and pants down, steps out of one trouser leg, then the other, kicks the garments out of the way and is now completely naked. His erection stands to attention, twitches a little under Watson's appreciative stare.

"You're still wearing your trousers," Holmes states, reproachful. "Why is that?"

"I was busy watching you." Watson opens the first button. "Care to help me with that?"

"Gladly."

Holmes sinks to his knees once more, a little more gracefully this time, grabs Watson by the hollows of his knees and pulls him forward. Watson huffs a little but lets it happen. It's only a matter of seconds until the buttons are open and Holmes reaches for the waistband.

"Ready?" he asks and Watson nods, lifts his hips obligingly and Holmes pulls the trousers down. Watson's erection catches in the fabric of his underpants and when freed, flops onto his belly with a sound that is both comical and obscene but Holmes is too preoccupied to pay much attention.

Watson's legs are long and muscular, his lower legs hairier than his thighs, and the injured left leg is thinner than the right one, thinner but no longer thin.

"What are you doing, Holmes," he asks when Holmes nudges his knees apart.

Holmes doesn't answer. It's a rhetorical question and no more worthy of a reply now than when it was asked for the first time, a little while back, right after Holmes licked Watson's sweat off his neck.

His curiosity is piqued and he feels his nostrils flare as he takes Watson's scent in. It's intense down here, woodsy and spicy, clean and musky, all at once and anything but unpleasant. Watson doesn't restrict his cleanliness to his hands and upper body; Holmes has listened to more than one enraged speech about personal hygiene and how washing oneself does wonders where disease prevention is concerned, and so he has no qualms as he leans forward to inspect what interests him so.

Watson's testes are hot and heavy when he takes them in hand, as if to judge their weight and overall condition. His own sac is looser than Watson's, but then, so is the rest of his body when compared to Watson's compact, strong build. Watson's cock is a thing of beauty and Holmes takes a moment to admire, sits back on his heels and just looks. A single drop sits at its tip, glistening in the sunlight that filters in through the shutters that are half closed in an attempt to prevent the room from getting too hot and he touches his middle finger to the tip to catch the drop before it rolls farther down. When he licks it off his finger to determine if it has a taste – it does: it's salty –, Watson makes a small, needy sound and changes his sitting position to one half lying and half propped up on his elbows.

Holmes knows what he'd like to do next, but will it be welcome? Yet here, at long last, is the chance he's been hoping for. The object of his desire is laid out before him to touch and, yes, to taste, and so Holmes lowers his head and licks along the thick shaft in one determined sweep of his tongue.

"Christ!" Watson's body all but arches off the bed. "Warn a man, will you!"

It doesn't sound as if the doctor objects to Holmes' experiment and so he continues his exploration, cradles the heavy sac in his hand and gives it a light squeeze. Then he zigzags his tongue from base to tip, sucks on the vein and swirls his tongue around the tip. The tip feels spongy against his tongue, but the skin of the cock itself is smooth and warm, soft even, very much in contrast to the steely hardness that's sheathed within.

Watson fists the sheets.

Thus encouraged, Holmes takes his experiment one step further and sucks the now glistening cockhead into his mouth, swallows as much of the thick length as he can before his gag reflex sets in. Watson lets go of the sheets and grabs a handful of Holmes' hair with a ferocity that is actually rather painful but Holmes pushes the feeling of discomfort aside because, frankly, he's quite overwhelmed by the fact that he has the power to elicit such a strong reaction. Watson's other hand flies to his mouth to muffle his moans.

Holmes lets go of Watson's cock when the moans become more urgent, and nudges him to shuffle up, directs him to the middle of the bed and follows him, crawling on his hands and knees. When Watson reaches for him, however, he swats his hands away.

"Not now," he murmurs between licks and bites. "Let me learn you first."

With a resigned sigh, Watson drops back against his pillow. He knows better than to interrupt one of Holmes' ongoing field studies and accepts his fate. Not at all unwillingly, judging by the sounds he makes.

Holmes quickly finds out that while Watson seems to enjoy being caressed with soft touches it's when he grows bolder, applying more pressure, gripping and kneading harder and more demanding, that Watson starts to squirm and writhe and his whimpers grow more and more urgent.

He's hesitant about touching the left leg at first, not wishing to intrude into an area that may be considered off limit, given its history, but Watson does not seem to mind when his fingers lightly skim across the scar tissue, and so he sets out to add these details to the map of Watson's body he's creating in his mind. He lets his hands travel across the marred flesh, carefully touches the twisted skin and finally lowers his head to lick along the angry red scar that zigzags from the inner thigh down and across the knee, kisses the smaller scars that are scattered everywhere, some of them sunken in, some puckered, all of them ugly and yet, they're unique and as much a part of Dr Watson as his beautiful hands and his aquiline nose.

Then Watson has had enough of being a passive participant in a game that's clearly intended for two, squirms out of the way and opens a drawer. When he finds what he's fumbling for he turns and holds up a small jar for Holmes to see. "Petroleum jelly," he says. "It will make some, uh, things a little easier." The expression in his eyes hovers between hopeful and uncertain.

Holmes knows what it is Watson is hinting at and as it's exactly what he wants, too, he says, "I want you inside me."

Watson blinks. "What was that?"

It's obvious he's missed a few steps in Holmes' decision-making process and so Holmes repeats, slowly and patiently, "I want you inside me. Please, John."

The jar drops to the mattress when Watson brings their mouths together in a crushing kiss. "God, Holmes – Sherlock," he finally says, gasping for breath. "You're –" he swallows. "I've dreamed about this for such a long time. Each night in the trenches, with only your letters to keep me from giving up. Wanting you so much and promising myself that if I ever made it back –" His voice threatens to break and he buries his face in the curve of Holmes' neck. "To have you like this, here," he kisses the sensitive spot where neck meets shoulder, "and that you should want me, too –"

"I've always wanted you," Holmes gently says and now that he's said it out loud, he knows it's the truth, plain and simple. "I've wanted you from the moment you told me you would only agree to share this flat with me if I removed my experiments from the dining table and you would not tolerate body parts in the kitchen."

Watson huffs out a small laugh. "I did say that, didn't I."

"You did. In a very stern voice. And I wanted you even more when you started taking boxing lessons and returned all sweaty and disheveled."

"Why did you never—" Watson makes a helpless gesture and Holmes shrugs.

"It's not exactly an easy subject to address," he says. "How was I to know if my advances would be welcome? You seemed happy enough to entertain the ladies."

"I see. Well, I do like the ladies, 's true, but I've always liked men better. And then I met you and only ever wanted you." He leans in and kisses Holmes. The kiss is soft but intense, full of longing. "Only you." He reaches for the jar, unscrews the lid and dips his fingers into the yellowish substance. "Are you sure about this? You don't have to, you know."

Holmes lies back and spreads his legs in wordless invitation. He's never been more certain about anything in his whole life, and he holds very still when the first finger enters him, slowly and carefully, and after a few nervous breaths he relaxes. It's not precisely painful but not very pleasurable either and he wonders how on earth he's supposed to take Watson's thick cock when one finger…

"Aaaaah, Christ."

"Like that?" Watson looks a little smug and Holmes opens his mouth for a retort when, "Bloody hell, do that again!" Watson twists his hand, crooks his finger and another jolt shoots through him. "Oh God yes! Again!"

Watson is only too happy to oblige and when he feels he has sufficiently prepared Holmes, he smears a generous portion of the jelly on his cock and settles himself between Holmes' legs.

"Ready?" he asks. His voice trembles and it's obvious that he's past waiting, only pulls himself together for Holmes' sake.

Holmes nods. "How do you want me?" he asks, a little uncertain. He's painfully aware of how limited his expertise is where certain bedroom activities are concerned.

"Like this," Watson says. "Exactly like this, so I can see you and kiss you, too." He brings himself into position and with what little must remain of his self-control, he asks one last time, "Are you absolutely sure? There'll be no turning back once we've passed this point."

"We're past turning back already," Holmes says. He wants this so bad he's starting to hurt. "Please –"

Whatever he's intended to say next turns into a gasp when he feels the blunt head of Watson's cock push inside. It's too big and it's so painful, he's stretched to a point he hasn't foreseen, has not thought possible, and no amount of preparation or petroleum jelly will ever get him ready for this… His whole body tenses.

"Shhh," Watson murmurs. "Breathe. It'll be alright in a minute." And he stops, kisses Holmes' throat. "Sherlock," he whispers, "oh God, Sherlock. All these years."

Holmes feels his body yield.

Watson slides all the way in.

When Watson starts moving, Holmes is ready. Watson is holding back at first, trying to be gentle. It's obvious even for someone as inexperienced as Holmes and it's not at all what he wants. He reaches Watson's hair, buries his hands in the thick chestnut strands.

87

"Harder, John."

And Watson starts fucking him in earnest. Holmes wraps his arms around Watson's shoulders, lifts his legs and wraps them around his waist. Watson holds himself up on his elbows, thrusting from his hips in smooth, steady strokes and his cock brushes past the spot inside Holmes that makes his vision fray around the edges. It's pure, unadulterated bliss.

"Harder," he pants. "Fuck me harder. Like that, yes. Don't stop." He grabs Watson's arse that is as firm and muscular as the rest of him and pulls him closer. "John, please."

Watson grunts something unintelligible, his hips thrusting into Holmes with brute force. The sound of flesh slapping against flesh is the filthiest and most exciting thing Holmes has ever heard and he cries out, feels his climax approach, and still Watson pounds into him.

"Touch yourself," Watson pants in between thrusts. "I can't –," he sounds as if he's in pain. "Fuck, you're so tight. So hot –" His voice trails off and he closes his eyes, squeezes them shut, makes a noise between a growl and a groan and the sound shoots through Holmes like liquid fire. He does as he's told, wraps his fingers around his cock and starts stroking himself in jerky, uncoordinated movements. Watson opens his eyes when he feels Holmes' hand move against his stomach and looks down.

"That's it," he gasps. "Sherlock. Yes."

It's all it takes. A wailing sound escapes Holmes' throat that would mortify him to the core at any other time but he's past caring. He feels his balls rise up against his body and his prick starts pulsing in his hand, shooting strings of creamy white along his belly, his chest. Above him, Watson does not miss a single beat, fucks him through his orgasm until he, too, loses his steady rhythm and comes with a hoarse shout and one last, brutal thrust. Holmes feels him twitch deep inside of him and his own spent prick gives one last, tiny shudder in response.

They cling to each other until their breath has returned to normal, then Watson carefully pulls out and drops to his side, facing him. Holmes is too tired to move and so he just lies there, legs spread, his stomach and chest smeared with his ejaculate, Watson's dribbling out of him. Neither is appealing but he cannot bring himself to move. But he does eventually manage to turn his head and meet Watson's eyes.

"Sherlock," Watson, no, *John*, murmurs. "You're so beautiful."

"Nonsense," he replies, feeling his ears grow hot. "You're lost in a post-coital haze. I'm not beautiful."

"Yes, you are." John reaches over and starts drawing circles into the sticky mess on Holmes' stomach. "You've always been handsome, in a detached and haughty way, but just now? You're gorgeous." He softly kisses the tip of Holmes' nose, then his lips. "I look at you, post-coital and all, and I know I never want to be with anyone else again."

Holmes reaches for John's hands and presses a kiss to his knuckles.

"Neither do I, John," he says. "Neither do I."

In the end it's John, forever the cleanly man of medicine, who gets up, limps to the corner where his cane is propped up against the wall, and goes to fetch a damp cloth so Holmes can clean himself up. He brings a towel, too, to cover the wet spot. When all is as neat as can be under the circumstances, he lies down again and pulls Holmes into his arms.

Holmes twines their fingers together and closes his eyes. His whole body hums in contentment.

"Bees," he murmurs sleepily.

John yawns. "What?"

"I never understood why anyone would speak of butterflies in one's stomach."

"I don't follow."

"Bees, that's what it is. Not some fluttering nonsense upsetting my digestive tract. When you're with me, there's a humming all the way from deep inside of me to my fingertips and down to my toes, like a swarm of bees."

"Mhm."

"A content, happy colony settling into its hive after a long day of swarming the fields gathering pollen."

"Yes, Sherlock. Bees. Got it. We'll find you that little house in the countryside you've been talking about forever and you can have ten hives there, if you want." He hugs Holmes closer and kisses his ear. "Now sleep, love. We have some catching up to do, you and I."

"On sleep?"

"On everything."

Across the street, the phonograph has finally stopped caterwauling and the last thing Holmes hears before he drifts off to sleep is the voice of their landlady, Mrs Hudson, bidding her weekly bridge group a cheerful good evening.

Nectar
By Narrelle M Harris

Sherlock Holmes had been brilliant as usual—right up until the point where he wasn't. He was a clever man, but sometimes humanity was more vicious and cruel than even his great mind could account for.

Doctor John Watson very kindly did not bring the glaring oversight up, once he'd regained consciousness from the tranquilising darts Mayer, a former city animal control officer, had used on them. Partly this was because Sherlock was slow to wake up, which concerned John deeply.

Mostly it was because they were now both chained and padlocked to the cast iron radiator embedded in the floor of a dilapidated house in what seemed to be an abandoned estate.

John's concern for his friend diminished a little when Sherlock awoke and immediately complained about the smell of their lodgings. He submitted to John's examination of his pulse rate and pupils. The chains binding them to the wall gave them at least that much movement.

"You'll live," was John's diagnosis.

"That remains to be seen." Sherlock sounded irritated with John and beyond disgusted with himself when he added, "How could I have been so *stupid*?"

"The escalation was extreme," John offered, "Who could have imagined Mayer would avenge a stolen painting by kidnapping a *child*? Or that he'd attempt to avenge himself on *us* when you uncovered his scheme?"

"No excuse."

John ignored him in favour of practical considerations. For the next several hours, they tested the limits of their prison.

The radiator was immovable, with the pipes embedded in the concrete floor and the feet of the unit also drilled into place. The heater itself was defunct, so they had no hope of warming the frigid room with it either.

The room itself was brick and concrete. The single high-up window, the glass of it broken into shards, showed that they were in a basement. No vehicles went by, nor could any be heard. A cat slunk past at one point, but it was the only sign of life.

John shouted for help anyway. If anyone heard, they didn't reply.

The steel chain binding them was slender but heavy, and there was a lot of it. It was also unbreakable. Attempts to use the radiator for leverage resulted in a few scratches on the links and both of them bruising their wrists to no good purpose.

John's hands were chained closely together, though his feet were free. He was positioned closest to the broken window, through which a bitter autumn wind curled periodically. John had sufficient lateral movement to reach it. On tiptoe, he could see only that they were in the middle of empty roads and fall-down houses. He could see a grey patch of sky.

He could by no means reach the closed door on the other side of the room.

Sherlock was hard by the wall. His hands were also close-chained together and to the radiator, so his range of movement was much more proscribed than John's.

Their shoes and belts were gone. Their watches too, and John thought it was as well he hadn't been armed, or Mayer may well have shot them both already.

The next five hours were annoying but tinged with the expectation that either Mayer would return for them (they had four plans for that) or, less likely, that Lestrade would track them down.

The *next* five hours, stretching as they did into the cold night, found John and Sherlock huddled together for warmth. Sherlock told John about some of his early cases to pass the time, including some excellent impersonations of his brother Mycroft, Detective Inspector Lestrade and his old chemistry professor, which reduced John to bouts of appreciative laughter, and reciprocal impressions of senior surgeons, and a haughty commanding officer who couldn't pronounce 'anaesthetise'.

The five hours after *that* were sleepless because of the aching cold and the hard floor; and the growing concern that they could be here for a very, very long time.

They made bad jokes. John talked about nights on Afghani mountainsides on deployment and friendly fire incidents. He said that tonight they might be freezing and hungry, but at least no-one was dropping bombs on them, not even the Americans.

Five more hours took them into the morning, slightly warmer, though their cold-shocked bodies could hardly tell the difference.

It looked like Mayer wasn't coming back.

That was a very big problem.

Sherlock looked at John, who was sitting with his wrists resting on his bent knees and staring at the floor.

"The human body can survive for three days without water. Sometimes longer."

John pursed his lips thoughtfully. "I knew someone who managed it for five. I'm afraid it was the hospital food that got him in the end."

"Humans can go for even longer without food."

"You clearly haven't noticed how irascible I get when I haven't eaten."

"I was too polite to mention it."

They laughed.

"Good thing I ate before we went out yesterday morning, then."

"Quite."

Sherlock hadn't, though. Focused as he was on the case, he hadn't ingested more than half a sandwich for two days. The last time he'd consumed liquid was the swallow of tea, yesterday morning.

Neither remarked on this. They were both acutely aware of it.

For the next twelve hours they called for help, together and separately. They tapped an SOS on the radiator in case the pipes led to someone who could hear on the upper floors. They examined the windows, floors, walls, for anything that might be of use—a nail to pick the padlock, for example—with no result.

Sherlock complained that the way they were chained meant he couldn't escape by dislocating his shoulder or breaking his thumb and wriggling out, as he'd done on prior occasions. John nodded and said, "Yeah, I know" as though it was something he'd also done before.

"Have you?"

"Once," John admitted, "It was a stupid practical joke my university roommate pulled. I dislocated my shoulder getting out of the damned ropes. If I'd been able to move any time in the next week, I'd have thrown him through a window."

"You're getting irascible."

"Yes, I am. What of it?"

"Nothing."

John sighed crankily. "I'd kill for a sandwich right now."

"If you gave me half I'd help you hide the body."

They laughed, even though their voices rasped.

After they'd been in the basement for thirty six hours, they weren't joking any more. Sherlock refused to discuss his symptoms but John knew them anyway: the decreased sweating; the onset of muscle cramps; the increased respiration and the incipient fever. Sherlock was more dehydrated than John, and was betraying the signs sooner. Neither of them was critical yet, but they were far from comfortable.

After everything they'd been through together, it began to look like this was how they'd die. Together. Of thirst.

In the thirty-seventh hour, the storm broke out.

Rain spattered through the open window onto John's face, waking him from a reverie that was more a stupor. He absently licked drops of water from his lips, and again: then his eyes were wide open. He lurched to his feet and staggered towards the window.

The pattering rain became a driving downfall. It ran in rivulets through the broken window.

John pushed his cheek against the wall, shoving the side of his mouth against a steady stream that gathered in a crack and poured down the bricks. Water flowed over his lips and tongue and down his dry, dry, dry throat. The water tasted of dust and brick and God knew what else, and it was the best water John had ever tasted in his life. He pooled a mouthful and swallowed it. Pooled a second. Swallowed it.

He tried to put his hands under the stream, but the chains wouldn't let him get that close. So he pooled a third mouthful, larger than the first two, and held it behind pressed lips.

He took two strides to Sherlock's side, dropped to his knees, and shook Sherlock awake.

Sherlock peered at him with weary perplexity. John tapped Sherlock's mouth with his fingers. When Sherlock didn't respond immediately, John poked his fingers between Sherlock's dry lips to part them, hovered—his mouth millimetres from Sherlock's—and then he opened his mouth to let the water dribble carefully down.

Sherlock made a small, desperate noise and swallowed the water. He tried to catch a spilled droplet with his tongue.

"Sorry," rasped John, "Had a full mouth and couldn't warn you. Wake up, now." He was already moving back to the wet bricks; the precious rivulet of rainwater.

After a small swallow, John filled his mouth and returned to Sherlock. He transferred the precious cargo into Sherlock's cupped hands. Sherlock was sucking at his wet fingers as John returned to the window; came back ready to fill Sherlock's palms again.

Sherlock tilted his head back. "Lose too much that way," he croaked, and opened his mouth.

London rained on them for an hour. It was almost like she wanted them to live. For an hour, John went back and forth, back and forth, back and forth. He drank sips almost as a by-product of collecting water for

Sherlock, and fed mouthful after mouthful of water to his friend. Buying time.

Sherlock revived a little with every mouthful, though his first strange thought on waking to John watering him mouth-to-mouth persisted.

What kind of flower actively feeds nectar to the bee?

The rain stopped, and John stopped, slumping in exhaustion beside Sherlock on the floor. They leaned against each other.

"Thank you."

"Don't thank me," laughed John, "You'll make me think we're not getting out of this."

Sherlock didn't say anything.

"You're welcome," said John.

*

As the forty-first hour was coming to a close, Lestrade and three of his constables broke the door down. A moment later, the ambulance crew arrived.

Lestrade was explaining how Mayer's son had finally broken down and told them about the abandoned property in a false name in Mile End, and his father's plan to keep 'those two nosy parkers out of my business.' They'd come straight from the interview room—just in time, by the look of it.

John started to laugh.

"Bet you're sorry you thanked me now," he said, full of irrepressible mirth, glad to be alive.

"This sort of thing never happens to Miss Marple," mock-complained Sherlock, and the two of them laughed like idiots.

*

At the hospital, John and Sherlock were given rehydration fluids, observed closely for a while and declared both medically fit and extremely lucky. Neither man listened closely beyond the doctor's pronouncement they could leave.

In the cab, they leaned against each other, half asleep, and only remembered when they got to Baker Street that their wallets were missing.

Mrs Hudson paid the fare without a word of complaint. She hovered rather, on their way upstairs to their flat, where they found she'd laid out sandwiches, cake and a pot of tea ready for their arrival.

"Call if you need anything," she offered. Sherlock might have been brusque about the fussing, except for the way her mouth was pursed and her eyes were red-rimmed. She really had been terribly worried about their disappearance.

"Dr Watson and I are fine, Mrs Hudson," he said.

"Thanks for the supper," said John, who always remembered the niceties. He took a bite of a cheese sandwich and made an effort not to cram it all in at once. He lifted the cup of tea she'd poured, took a grateful gulp, then saluted her with the cup as she left.

The next sandwich, John wolfed down. Still chewing, he took off his grubby coat and shirt and sat on the sofa in his jeans and vest, barefoot. He continued swigging tea and stuffing down sandwiches like there was no tomorrow.

Sherlock paced the room, filled with a strange, restless energy.

"Eat," insisted John, holding up the plate of sandwiches.

Sherlock picked up a triangle and bit into it, and found he was ravenous. He jammed the whole thing in his mouth and hardly chewed before swallowing. His circuit of the living room brought him past the plate again, and he snatched up three more sandwiches in his long hands and ate them in rapid succession.

By the next circuit, John had moved onto the apple tea cake. The sponge moist and rich, the apple baked to retain just a little firmness, the top of it crusted with sugar granules and cinnamon. A whole wedge had vanished and he was onto his second.

Sherlock wheeled around the room again, not touching the cake.

"Sit. You're making me dizzy," complained John.

"Eat your cake."

John ate his cake. Swigged tea. Sagged against the sofa, exhausted.

"Bloody hell," he said. Then he laughed. "I'm full as a boot."

"Hardly a surprise." Sherlock waved at the wreckage of sandwich platter and cake.

"Sod off," but John was grinning. He took a huge bite from a third slice of cake, then pulled a childish face at Sherlock. He washed the cake down with a giant gulp of tea and then simply sat there, replete, no longer thirsty or hungry, no longer steeling himself for a long, horrible death. For watching Sherlock suffer the same fate.

His mind let go of it all—the driving fear, the desperation to keep Sherlock alive at any cost—and his body lost its tension. Still holding a half piece of cake in one hand, a cup resting on his thigh in the other, John fell asleep, sagging into the cushions like a deflating air bed.

On the next circuit of the room, Sherlock paused in front of his sleeping flatmate to consider the scene. He leaned over to remove the precariously balanced half cup of tea and place it on the coffee table. Bent over John like that, Sherlock hesitated again.

Sugar and crumbs clung to the side of John's mouth. They clung to the hand that still held a fragment of apple teacake in the loose curl of his fingers.

Sherlock sat on the edge of the coffee table, stilled in his endless pacing at last, and looked at sleeping John.

What kind of flower actively feeds nectar to the bee?

Where had that come from?

Ridiculous.

We both could have died because of my mistake.

Well, the origins of *that* thought were clear enough at least, and very much steeped in fact.

John, who could have died and was instead asleep on their sofa, snuffled in his sleep, clutching at a bit of cake, looking boyish and vulnerable, even though he was tough and clever.

Sherlock reached for John's hand, the one that held the cake, and he carefully turned the hand palm up to extract the piece. Once he had it, Sherlock, on impulse, shoved the cake in his own mouth. It tasted…warm.

He still held John loosely by the wrist; John's fingers were dotted with cake crumbs and sugar.

Sherlock stared at those fingers. He stared at John's sleep-smoothed face. He stared at John's mouth, which had fed him water for a whole desperate hour. (*What kind of flower actively feeds nectar to the bee?*)

John's sugary fingers twitched in Sherlock's gentle hold, drawing Sherlock's attention again.

What Sherlock did next was another impulse. It was the flavour of the warm fragment of cake in his mouth, and the ease of John's wrist resting in Sherlock's palm; it was John's vulnerable expression in sleep and it was the knowledge of coming too close to the edge today, of taking John there with him, of the good luck of London rain, and John bringing them safe away from the precipice once more. It was exhaustion and relief and concern and guilt and awareness that it might all have ended today, with so much unsaid and undone. It was impulse and it was want, too. It was *want*.

It was an impulse, but when Sherlock moved, he did it slowly and with deliberation.

Sherlock lifted John's hand to his mouth, and with infinite care, he lipped at the tip of John's thumb. He licked it. He felt the granules of sugar, the fine rich crumbs of cake, and he sucked the pad of that thumb clean.

John, in his sleep, smiled, and his other fingers waved a tiny patting motion, bumping against Sherlock's upper lip and the side of his mouth. John said, "Hmmmm" and slept on.

Sherlock then lipped John's index finger, cleaning it of the remnants of cake. Sherlock closed his eyes, reveling in the texture of it, in the taste of sugar and skin. John's skin.

John hummed and patted against Sherlock's mouth with feathery fingertips again. He sighed contentedly and settled.

Sherlock's breathing deepened and in increments his body gave up its tension, too. He was so tired. So tired. The case was over, the danger was over, and they were alive. John was alive. And Sherlock was suddenly almost too tired to move.

John's fingers patted his mouth, which was still wrapped around sugary skin. John's sleepy voice said

"Mmmm", like he was content, and it made Sherlock feel…safe; and content, too.

Sherlock slipped John's middle finger between his lips and he sucked softly at it. He tasted sugar and cake and John. His eyes closed and his busy mind buzzed to quiet. After four days without sleep, after nearly but not dying, his body told him *sssshhhhh*, and he dozed.

*

For a few minutes, John dreamed a truly epic, erotic dream involving rain and Sherlock and kissing, and then coming because a great black wolf was licking his fingers.

He awoke, languid and happy, to the oddest sensation that the dream hadn't ended.

Blearily, he opened his eyes, and for a moment he didn't know what he was seeing. And then he knew, and was breathless with the wonder of it.

Sherlock, very clearly asleep, was sitting on the coffee table beside him, John's fingers in his mouth, suckling slightly.

John didn't move. He merely watched, considering; thinking about things he'd tried for years now to repress, believing such desires to be futile.

He thought about his efforts this day to ensure the person who mattered most to him survived; about forty-one hours spent trying not to regret all the things he'd never get to say or ask or do if they never escaped from that basement.

John watched Sherlock sleeping and suckling on his fingers. He thought how young Sherlock looked. Vulnerable, and a bit blissed out. Sherlock rarely looked like that awake. John liked it. He liked Sherlock's young-looking face, he liked his mouth, he liked

Sherlock's mind and his poor attempts to pretend he didn't have a heart; and a large heart, too. Sherlock was passionate about science, about music, about justice: that much John knew; that much John longed for—to be the target of some of that passion.

John thought he should extract his fingers from Sherlock's sleeping, sucking mouth, but he really didn't want to. He really, really didn't want to. Just a moment longer. One moment longer. It would be…

Sherlock's eyes opened. His expression was softly content at first and then alarmed, as he woke fully. He pulled away.

It was impulse, what John did next. Impulse and *want*. He caught Sherlock by the wrist. The grip could easily be broken, but the pressure was firm and deliberate.

But what to do next? John didn't want to say *I don't mind*, though he didn't. He didn't want to say *don't stop,* though he didn't want Sherlock to stop. He didn't want to say a word in case they were the wrong words.

Instead his gaze met Sherlock's and John's always so readable face said *yes* and *please* and *it's okay* and *I like it* and *stay*. His expression was kind and hopeful and yearning and resigned and understanding and wanting and ready for anything or nothing.

Sherlock stopped withdrawing. He *stayed*. He read John's face, line by line, all the hidden things that weren't hidden any more. For long, long moments they looked at each other, and conversations took place in the silence, rising and setting like the turn of the sun in their eyes.

And slowly, in answer to all the things he read in John's expressive face, Sherlock leaned forward to lick again, at John's fourth finger, still with crumbs clinging to the skin.

John sighed, happy-content-hopeful. Then he said, "You've got… sugar… on your..." He gestured towards Sherlock's lip.

Sherlock blinked.

"I could… help you with that."

Sherlock gave the shortest and sharpest of nods.

John pressed a finger to the single grain of sugar clinging to the fullness of Sherlock's lower lip, collecting it against the groove of his own fingerprint. He swallowed hard, then tilted his finger slightly towards Sherlock's mouth. An offering.

Nothing happened.

John tried not to be disappointed. He tried not to feel as though this was his first and last chance and he'd somehow blown it.

Sherlock tilted his head ever-so-slightly, leaned forward a fraction, and settled his lips over John's finger. He sucked at it, gently.

John's breath hitched and then he watched, mesmerised, until Sherlock pulled delicately away.

"You, also…" began Sherlock boldly, and becoming suddenly hesitant, "On your. Mouth. Might I… return the service?"

John nodded, never taking his gaze from Sherlock's.

Sherlock in slow turn pressed his finger to the corner of John's mouth, bringing away crumbs and cinnamon. John drew Sherlock's fingertip between his lips. Licked. Sucked at the pad.

His heart was hammering.

Sherlock leaned towards him now, and pressed his lips to that same spot at the side of John's mouth. John felt the tip of Sherlock's tongue sneak out, swipe against his skin, and then John couldn't wait any longer. He turned his head to meet Sherlock's mouth.

The wisp of pressure was all there was for a moment, and then a little more, and then Sherlock's lush lips were pressed right up against John's. John parted his a little and the very tip of his tongue licked another sweet crumb from a full lip, and then, and then…

Oh, that kiss. Hesitant, then not. Shy, then not. Soft then hard. The familiar suddenly unfamiliar, and after the strangeness, beautifully familiar again. They knew each other, and this was just a new way to know, after all.

"The myriad ways in which this could be a bad idea," murmured Sherlock against John's lips, "Have doubtless already occurred to you."

"Yes," murmured John back, "But right now all I can think is what a fantastic idea it is. Brilliant. Like you." He kissed Sherlock again, wanting to know more of the familiar in this new way.

Sherlock deepened the kiss, until he paused to say, "Yes. Brilliant. This is a brilliant idea. If I'd known you thought it was too, I'd have done something sooner."

John's hands smoothed over Sherlock's shoulders and around his back; Sherlock pulled John close. He was discovering that John, properly motivated, was a superb kisser.

They parted briefly for a breath, to shift, to caress skin and hair. Then there was too much space between them, and they were in each other's arms. Sherlock might have been pushing John across the sofa to sprawl across him, except that John was also pulling him down on top. John might have been wrapping legs and arms around Sherlock to anchor him, except that Sherlock, with a hand under John's thigh and another around

John's ribs, was encouraging John to hook a leg over his hip, and arm around his back. Give and take. Push and pull. Yes and please.

"Don't let this be another dream," John murmured before kissing a line across Sherlock's jaw and down his throat.

Sherlock laughed breathily. "Oh, John. Consider the evidence." He rolled his hips against John's, their erections under their clothes pressing together.

John's eyes sparkled and he pushed against the glorious roll of Sherlock's hips. "Yes. I see. Evidence. Evidence is good."

Sherlock pulled John's vest down to mouth at throat, nipples, the scar of the old wound. When the fabric refused to stretch further, he shoved it up, out of the way. His lips and tongue worked first one peaking nipple, then the other. John arched into the sensation, fingers carding through Sherlock's dark hair, then he brought Sherlock up for a kiss.

His mouth, John thought, *that lavish mouth. All that genius, all that passion, so much life in it, that mouth. Oh god. Your beautiful mouth.*

Sherlock sucked lightly on John's lower lip, pressed deep kisses into the heat of John's mouth. Gloried in the heat and wet and warmth of it.

That mouth, Sherlock thought, *that gave me water. That gives me praise. That laughs with me. That gives and gives to me. God. Yes. John. Your mouth.*

"We have a dilemma," said Sherlock at last. The frisson of worry in John's expression prompted a continuation. "I want to continue this in the bedroom." John grinned. Legs clamped around Sherlock's waist, he thrust his hips against Sherlock's. Sherlock grinned back. "Exactly." He kissed John again. "More room. Much more comfortable. But-"

"But?"

"I don't want to stop long enough to get there."

John ran his fingers through Sherlock's hair again, and they kissed again, and John said: "Do you think I'm going to change my mind between here and there?"

Sherlock decided he had best confess it. "The thought had crossed my mind."

"I won't if you won't." John said it lightly, but there was that frisson of worry again.

"I won't," said Sherlock quietly, "I almost waited too long already."

Mouths met again, in a long kiss, starting tender, building in need and heat until, with a breathless laugh, John unhooked his legs and shoved playfully at Sherlock's shoulder. "Race you there."

Sherlock made it to the room a half second ahead of John. Hands about John's waist, John's hands about his, they half flung each other onto the bed. Laughing, they stripped, attempts to help each other a delightful hindrance that neither minded.

Then they were naked, John sitting astride Sherlock's hips, grinding down, until Sherlock wrapped his arms around John's torso and pulled him down into more hot kisses. He turned them so that he was on top again. Without clothes barring the way, he licked and kissed and sucked John's skin. John's hands were in his hair, guiding him, throat to belly, nipple to hip. *Brilliant.*

John surged up again to mouth at Sherlock's throat, his sternum, each peaked nipple, his shoulders and arms and hands, across to his flat, pale stomach. Everywhere his mouth touched, Sherlock arched his body into that wonderful heat.

Am I the bee or the flower?

Sherlock dismissed the useless thought.

Sugary tongue-tips met and twined. They shared warm breaths and as they kissed, they tangled themselves in each other's limbs, hips finding a rhythm, hard pricks pushing against each other, leaving bare skin slick and slippery. Cocks hard and wet; hips moving, pushing, and pressing; mouths sucking and kissing; hands caressing and clutching; breath sighing then panting and moaning and grunting and then, *God, yes yes yesyesyes.*

Afterwards, John lay flat on his back, grinning at the ceiling. Sherlock lay flat on his back beside him, with a more speculative expression. He rolled to wrap himself around John's body, stickiness be damned, leg hooked over John's, arm across his chest. He didn't ask if it was all right. Of course it was all right. John's whole body told him so, with the vibration of a happy laugh in his chest; the hand that rubbed proprietarily across Sherlock's arm and the other curved around his back; the wriggle of his toes before settling; the press of those lips against the crown of Sherlock's head.

"Must remember to thank Mrs Hudson for the cake," murmured John, entirely too smugly.

Sherlock lifted his arm long enough to take John's hand, hold it to his mouth and to suck on one of his fingers. No sweetness left, except for the taste of John himself, which was enough. John kissed his hair again, and waved his fingers slightly, patting at Sherlock's face, as he'd done in his sleep.

"Sherlock," said John.

"Mmm?" Sherlock suckled on one, then two, of John's fingers.

"Do you realise that bastard Mayer still has our shoes?" And he laughed, a free and happy sound, which set Sherlock to laughing with him.

John nuzzled against Sherlock's fine, dark hair. Sherlock resumed suckling on John's fingers. Although he couldn't see John's expression, he was aware of how it changed, from puzzled to pleased to content.

And that's how they slept, naked and wrapped close, John with his nose in Sherlock's hair; Sherlock with John's fingers in his mouth. Connected, as always, but in new ways. Different but equal; thirsting and quenching; needing and giving in perfect balance.

A Prodigious Infestation
By Jamie Ashbird

"Holmes. Why the devil is the window open?" Watson shook out his coat.

"Thank the lord you're back, Doctor Watson," Mrs Hudson grumbled. "He refuses to shut it."

Holmes ambled into the room, an unlit pipe in his mouth.

"Do shuffle off, Mrs Hudson. And shut the door behind you."

That she did, though not without a damning glare.

Like coils released the two men drew close, breathed each other in with sealed lips.

"I missed you, dearest fellow."

"Your sojourn agreed with you, John. Or was it three days away from me? Either way you've a rosy glow."

"I know a way to keep it there," John smiled. "But first, what mischief was I not here to prevent?"

Holmes bent at the knees, his gleaming eyes level with his John's. "Come and see." He took John's hand and pulled him to his room. "Up there."

John stared at a pale semicircle hanging from the cornice. He narrowed his eyes, hoping he was imagining the crawling movements. "Sherlock?"

"I found a queen, John."

"Found?"

Sherlock shrugged. "Bought. Found. It's all the same."

"I've no doubt I should be angrier than I am," John gave him a fond smile.

"Ah, but we've an infestation," Sherlock wound his arms around his dear doctor's waist, "I shall have to beg to share your bed."

Little Cupid
By Lucy Jarsdell

"—given the rarity of such high temperatures, doctors are warning their patients to take measures to prevent heat exhaustion. These include drinking plenty of water, staying in the shade during—"

The sound of the radio melted into garble for a few moments as John slid down in the bathtub to immerse his head under the water. The cool ripples of it lifted his hair away from his scalp, separating the clumps it had formed into from the incessant sweat of the day. Eyes scrunched closed, he shook his head from side to side, enjoying the sensation, the near chilliness, then released his breath from his nostrils and sat back up.

"—treating patients for severe burns after some ill-advised sunbathing on car roofs. Hopefully, all of you out there have the sense to lie on a towel. And to use tanning lotion, of course! And with meteorologists predicting even higher temperatures over the next few days, it's looking certain that this heat wave will be one of the things for which 1976 goes down in history."

The bathroom window was open, and over the blather of the radio, John could hear the traffic going past, shouts from the drivers more noticeable than usual thanks to open windows and heat-induced irritability. Also, of course, he could hear music drifting from other homes, the chatter and laughter of the people sitting at hastily set out tables outside cafes, the more pleasant sounds of summer in the city.

It was extraordinary how much he'd missed London in the years he'd been away with the army. Even more extraordinary, of course, that he'd lost his resistance to the heat so fast. Years spent in deserts, living and fighting in intense heat, and now a British summer heat wave had him running for a cool bath.

He was lounging back in the lukewarm water, calm and contented, listening to a passenger argue with the driver of the 74 bus outside, when another noise intruded into his ears.

Zzzzzzz

It was very quiet, so quiet that he almost thought it was just in his imagination. But no, there it was again.

Zzzzzzzzzzzzzzz

He opened his drooping eyelids to study the room and spotted immediately the source of the annoying, penetrative sound. A little buzzing insect hurtling around near the ceiling. A bee.

Why the silly bloody creatures couldn't find the open window again after they'd already flown through it, he didn't know. Surely it was easier to pick out an open window from among all the things in a small room than it was to pick it out from the whole of Baker Street.

It was probably time to get out of the bath anyway, John thought with a sigh. The bee continued to blunder its way around the bathroom as he heaved himself to his feet, scooped water off his skin, and stepped out onto the bath mat.

"—literally gallons of sun tan lotion sold over the last 72 hours, and many shops running low on supplies, means a lot of—"

Confused beyond all capacity to navigate, the bee bumped into his right shoulder, bounced off, and began another round of high speed laps.

Zzzzzzzzzzzzzzzzzzzzzzzz

"Damn it," John muttered under his breath. He wasn't a fan of insects, and would quite happily have swatted it, except for the fact that Sherlock was particularly fond of bees. Not that Sherlock was even in the house, but...well. John was particularly fond of Sherlock, wasn't he? Not that Sherlock was even aware…

John was in the middle of toweling himself off when the stripy little moron bumped off his left buttock and then flew into the mirror above the sink, and really, that was just annoying. John dropped his towel, tipped his and Sherlock's toothbrushes out of the chipped whiskey glass by the sink, and turned his attention to catching the bee.

"—counts being far higher than usual leading to misery from hay fever sufferers—"

Of course, catching a bee in a glass is a lot easier if the bee ever bloody lands.

"—scientists believe it will help to enliven the flagging population of bumblebees in the South East, which—"

This one didn't seem inclined to land anywhere. It also didn't appear to be flagging. It was almost like it was taunting him. It would skim past the top of the cabinet or the cistern at a leisurely pace, testing the surface with its spindly little legs, and then just as John was poised to slam the glass down over it—whoosh!— the little sod was gone again.

Then, disaster. Turning to try and follow the erratic path of the bee, John bashed his elbow on the door handle. Which not only made his arm go all weird, it also popped the door open.

The bee hadn't been able to find the open window, but it sure as hell didn't miss the door.

Had he not been alone in the house, John probably would have thought twice about the wisdom of chasing a bee around while naked and still fairly damp. Happily however, he knew that Mrs Hudson was at her sister's and Sherlock was off arguing with somebody at the National Library, and he was safe to pursue his quarry without having to pause and put on a towel.

Out of the bathroom, and the bee teasingly paused on the frame of a picture for just long enough that John was inches away with the glass poised, before it buggered off again.

Zzzzzzzzzzzzzzz

The drone of the radio was still audible from the bathroom, but John was only interested in the sound of the bee. This was starting to feel personal now. He was affronted. That bee was going in the glass and then it was going out the window. End of! Captain John Watson would be triumphant!

Almost giggling, John thundered into the kitchen in his pursuit, nearly caught the bee when it landed on the hob but succeeded only in adding another chip to the rim of the glass, then had to stand and stare around to try and find it again.

The next time it passed through his field of vision, it was going through into the living room, and John followed after, bare feet slapping on the tile floor, skidding on the carpet, and there was the bee, right there, perched on the corner of the mantelpiece, perfectly lined up. John stretched out his arm, brought it down and, with a dull thud of glass on wood, the bee was trapped. John raised his arms above his head and bobbed up and down on the balls of his feet, a little victory dance.

And that's when he realised that his earlier assertion that he was alone in the house was, in fact, incorrect.

"What..." Sherlock's voice said, sounding somewhat choked. And well he might, for though he and John knew one another very well by this point, John was quite aware that Sherlock had never seen him perform a victory dance over a captured insect before, let alone a naked victory dance.

For a moment, John froze. But only for a moment. Then, pulling his dignity about himself with care, he turned to face the direction from which Sherlock's voice had come, and tried to affect a normal posture and facial expression.

"Hallo Sherlock, when did you get back?"

Sherlock, in his armchair with his legs curled up under him and a large book open in his lap, stared at John with wide eyes and an uncharacteristically blank expression.

"I...the librarian...terrible bore...took the volume...without permission...bus..."

John watched that expressive face shift and twitch as Sherlock tried to work out whatever was going on in his thoughts.

"You're naked," was what he came up with, after some contemplation.

"Yes, I was having a bath," John said, refusing to let any note of apology creep into his voice. "I chased after a bee that got in through the window." He gestured to the glass on the end of the mantel, in which the bee was bumping about in confusion.

"But you're…" Sherlock squinted at him, tilted his head back and forth with his eyes still fixed on John, swept him up and down with his gaze, and finally frowned hard, something of his normal alert expression returning to his face.

Never had John more strongly wished that he was clothed.

"What's wrong?" he asked gamely, folding his arms over his chest.

"I...hm." Sherlock lifted the book out of his lap and stared down at where it had lain. Without looking back up at John, he said clearly and portentously, "John, I believe I have an erection."

John just didn't know what to say about that.

"It..." Sherlock continued after a moment. "It just turned up."

A little splurt of laughter bubbled up inside John and escaped through his lips. Sherlock frowned at him.

"What caused it?" Sherlock demanded.

"How do you expect me to know? I'm not in charge of what happens in your pants!"

"Well, I haven't had one in years, and now suddenly it pops up as soon as you come charging into the living room and...oh!"

Moving slowly so as not to draw further attention, John reached out, picked up a cushion off the nearby sofa, and held it in front of his crotch.

"John, am I attracted to you?" Sherlock demanded.

Now, John Watson has always considered himself an open-minded man. A young man during the era of the sexual revolution, he's seen his share of life. And he had recognised early on that he occasionally noticed nice-looking men in the same way he did nice-looking women. He had long since recognised that he noticed *Sherlock* the way he noticed nice-looking women.

But you know what? Sherlock wasn't supposed to notice back. Because Sherlock was a great friend and a great flatmate and completely uninterested in sex or romance and his only crush had been on a woman, so

118

John could notice him all he liked and never have to worry about losing a friend or a living situation to some sort of romantic cock up.

And now Sherlock was staring at him like he was about to shout 'Eureka.'

"There are any number of reasons a man might get an erection, Sherlock," John said in his most doctorly tones. "Maybe something you were reading about—"

"I'm reading about fungal spores," Sherlock interrupted. "I've often read about fungal spores, and I've never reacted to them with arousal before. I think I am, John. I think I'm attracted to you."

"But...uh, why only now? We've lived together for over two years. Surely you'd have noticed before?" John said desperately.

"I've never seen you naked before, of course," Sherlock announced. "It makes perfect sense."

Sherlock rose from the chair and stood, book still held loosely in one hand.

"I've never looked closely at male bodies," he muttered with annoyance. "Stupid of me. I limited my studies to the female form, and when they produced no effect, I surmised that there was no effect to be had. Poor reasoning on my part, but I'll not make that mistake again!"

"So you are attracted to men," John surmised neatly, clutching the sofa cushion and glancing around for something with a bit more coverage. "I'm...I'm glad you've had this revelation, Sherlock. I'm sure I'll do my best to introduce you to some, uh, some nice chaps…"

He trailed off on noticing an apron hanging off the handle of the nearby kitchen door, and he dropped the cushion to make a grab for it, then pulled it haphazardly around himself. Unfortunately, as he did so, he took his eyes off his flatmate. And when he looked up again, said flatmate was suddenly a great deal closer than he had been before.

"John," Sherlock said in a low, worried tone," I've never been attracted to somebody before. What do I do?"

John's hands, in the middle of tying a bow behind his back, stilled. He stared, mouth open, at Sherlock's face. Sherlock's face which was, normally, so composed and severe, now worried. Off balance. Vulnerable.

John reached out and laid his hands on Sherlock's upper arms.

"Now look," he said gently. "If you're attracted to me, that's fine. I'd be lying if I said that that wasn't mutual, you're a good-looking man."

Rather than smiling at the compliment as he had hoped, Sherlock proceeded to look only more lost. The book slipped out of his fingers and thumped onto the floor

"But if we were to start anything," John continued, "well...things would change."

"Change? What would change? How?"

"Our...our relationship. We're very good friends, Sherlock. And we work well together, live well together." John gulped. "We...I...that's important. Maybe you don't want to change it."

Sherlock stared at him, hard, a frown creasing his pale forehead, head tilted quizzically to one side. "You've known that to happen," he said quietly.

John looked away.

"Kathleen," Sherlock murmured. "No. Jacinta, no. Kelly, unlikely."

John stared, gobsmacked, as Sherlock began to list every girl he'd ever so much as gone on a date with, in chronological order.

"Doris, no. Jilly, possibly...no. Frances—"

John flinched.

"Frances. Ah yes, you worked with her. And you changed jobs after you broke up. Left the hospital for your practice. I'm right, aren't I John?"

It was no use denying it. "I don't want that to happen to us," John said weakly.

"It might not."

"But it might!" His voice sounded thick to his own ears, the back of his throat squashing his words up tight, and Sherlock was looking at him with that terrible way he had, sympathy without pity, realisation without judgment, that always made John ache in the pit of his stomach.

"Sherlock, you like what we have, don't you? Why would you risk that?"

Sherlock stared at him, unmoving, for several very long seconds. Then he raised his hands to cup John's bare shoulders, John's hands still laid on his own arms.

"I like what we have very much," he said. "But I have the distinct feeling that it could...further develop. And we would still find much to value."

John squeezed his eyes shut. "You want to be...what? Lovers? Sherlock, that would be hard, on both of us. And—"

"You are my favourite person," Sherlock said simply, earnestly, and John just stared at him.

"Your...your favourite…"

"And you are brave, John. I know you are. Please."

John looked at Sherlock's face, took in the flush of emotion on his cheeks and the quiet intent of his

121

expression. Sherlock had worked something out, had theorised and tested and proven, and John had never doubted Sherlock when he wore this expression. Sherlock was sure. He was *sure*.

Who was John to argue with the second most intelligent man in London? Honestly, he didn't even want to. And honestly, though it sounded like something he would have said at five-years-old, Sherlock was his favourite person too.

John tugged Sherlock closer, stretched up the few inches that made the difference between their heights, and touched their lips together. Sherlock drew in a sharp breath, paused, and leaned into John, just a little, just enough.

A short, chaste little bit of a kiss, but it had John's heart thudding in his chest.

Carefully, so as not to startle, he took his hands from Sherlock's arms, moved them to his waist instead, and held him, drew him in closer. Sherlock followed easily, his eyes flickering open but his lips never leaving John's, and in a few slow moments they were holding each other, as close to one another as they'd ever been.

In the warm muggy room, pressed close with all of their body heat, the increased warmth of excitement, it felt almost overwhelmingly hot, sweat prickling on John's back in spite of the cool bathwater that hadn't even dried yet. He pressed closer still, slipping his hands underneath the back of Sherlock's shirt and splaying his palms on his skin.

Sherlock made a sweet little squeak of enjoyment against John's lips. He still had an erection, John could feel it.

More than that he could feel something new here, something almost tangible, a different kind of energy, taking that spark that existed between them when they worked together and building on it, dragging it into a new shape.

Their lips parted, and Sherlock drew back, looking at John with delight and astonishment, a high colour lighting up his narrow face. "John," he said quietly, and John waited for him to say more, but that seemed to be all Sherlock had wanted to say.

John.

"I think this could be...you're right," John said haltingly. "This could be the beginning of something even better."

Sherlock smiled tenderly, eyes sweeping over the features of John's face, over his neck and bare shoulders, then back to meet his eyes, quietly asking permission as his hand reached to the small of John's back, and tugged loose the tie of the apron.

John snorted and, not to be left behind, reached up to pop open the top button of Sherlock's shirt.

"We could go to bed, if you'd like," he offered, and Sherlock's face flushed further as he gave an awkward nod.

"Yes, I...let's, yes."

John grinned and stepped back from him, only to have his attention caught by the little sound of the bee bumping about in the glass. Odd, but he felt rather grateful to it now. As Sherlock moved past him towards the stairs, he reached out and righted the glass, letting the little bee buzz its way out again.

With the bee humming its way around the living room and the faint sound of the radio now playing pop songs in the bathroom; with the sunshine from the windows picking out the warm brown tones of Sherlock's hair and the delicate veins beneath his untanned skin; with a smile on his face and happiness tickling his insides, John followed Sherlock to the stairs, leaving the apron sprawled across the floor.

Unseen, the bee flew immediately to the open window and exited without a fuss, zooming away into the warm afternoon.

The Case Of The Poison Bees
By Kimber Camacho

Sherlock Holmes, consulting detective and occasional apiology lecturer, had been working since dawn in his laboratory, never changing out of his dressing gown and his favourite pair of tattered slippers. His partner John Watson, ex-army doctor and frequent medical consultant to one Sherlock Holmes, had been threatening easily once every month since they'd moved in together to burn the aged footwear or hide it under Mrs. Hudson's mulch pile in their shared garden. Had Sherlock taken him seriously, there might have been a row, but he had learned early on to know when John was serious about something.

A warm hand curved around the back of Sherlock's neck, just about the time he belatedly registered having heard familiar footsteps shuffling through the kitchen and down the steps to his lab, which once had been a dining room. That the other presence hadn't registered sooner was due to that familiarity; after nearly a year, even Sherlock's vigilant subconscious had begun to accept John as a fixture in his life.

"Did you get much sleep after I dropped off?" John asked, massaging lightly with his fingers for a moment before kissing the nape of Sherlock's neck. His nose tickled the fine straight hairs at the back of Sherlock's head.

"Hours and hours," Sherlock lied distractedly as he let one drop of amber liquid fall from his pipette onto the insect gently held atop a glass slide by tiny stretchy straps of Sherlock's own devising. The point was to avoid harming the bee while performing his experiments, and he'd smoke-doped the bee before he started, in order to keep it placid.

"Yeah, bollocks," John said fondly, a smile in his tone, smoothing back some strands of Sherlock's jet black hair from his forehead. "I had to fall for the only bloke who gets up at the crack of dawn to get his bee bondage on."

Rolling his eyes, Sherlock let out a sigh that sounded more aggrieved than he actually was. "You and your filthy mind," he muttered, moving the bee on the slide carefully under the microscope.

"You love my filthy mind," John reminded him with another kiss to his nape before sauntering into the kitchen, calling back easily, "Coffee? Tea? Anything?"

"Coffee, please," Sherlock called back, jotting down a few words in his notebook. He was gently dabbing the bee dry with a swab when a mug and then John's arm appeared in his peripheral vision. "Thank you," Sherlock murmured, gently returning the bee to the little enclosure on his lab table before turning to take up the mug and sip cautiously. John leaned against the table, his own mug in one fist and his rust-brown brows high in silent query. Smiling, Sherlock said a little loftily, "Yes, I've solved it."

Chuckling, John lifted his mug in a sort of toast. "Of course you did, it involves your two favourite things: crime solving and bees. Suppose you had a breakthrough when you woke up earlier?" Sherlock merely nodded; putting on gloves that went up to the elbow and carefully sliding back the fine mesh lid before reaching into the bee enclosure to scoop up a different bee. John made a rolling gesture with his mug, though without sloshing his coffee. "Well?"

A hint of a smile stole across Sherlock's somewhat stern features as he carefully restrained the second bee. "Quite ingenious, actually," he said, happy to explain, knowing John was genuinely interested. The man's amber-brown eyes looked even lighter with the late morning light coming in through the row of windows on the far wall, and Sherlock stole a glance at his lover's body as he spoke. "If Boris' death is proved accidental—such as a bee sting causing fatal anaphylaxis—then his sister Belinda, and by extension her husband, inherit his fortune. However, Boris Hendrick wasn't allergic to bee stings."

John's brows rose at this, his mouth falling open slightly as he waited for more. Sherlock's grey gaze flickered down and then up, taking in John's whole form, his reactions to the sight caught in that grey area between everything being new and everything being familiar; thing was, Sherlock didn't dread the latter, as he liked the idea of knowing everything about John Watson. Either unaware or not minding being subtly ogled, John had paused with his mug halfway to his mouth, obviously trying to figure out the importance of Hendrick's lacking an allergy. The thoughtful expression on his superficially ordinary features revealed to Sherlock the sensuality of slightly pursed well-formed lips, the firm strength in his jaw, the noble slope of his nose, marginally spread at the nostrils, and the ghost of a cleft barely indenting his chin; at a glance John Watson seemed fairly unremarkable, but Sherlock had found him intriguingly handsome upon further study. In point of fact, the man was one of the more important of Sherlock's ongoing studies.

Currently, Sherlock's favourite object of regular perusal was shirtless beneath his old green toweling robe, his skin buff-brown in contrast to the milky pale of Sherlock's, and his pyjama bottoms a dark olive drab reminiscent of army fatigues. It was a testament to John's trust in and affection for Sherlock that he was shirtless, as he had initially been a bit self-conscious of the scarring on his left shoulder, a permanent reminder of the incident which had sent John home from Afghanistan. Sherlock hadn't seen that scar, or the one high up on John's left thigh, until a few weeks after they'd become lovers; those scars had only made him more appreciative of the man's perseverance and strength of character. Over the months since he'd moved in, John had got into better shape and very nearly banished the limp he'd suffered since IED shrapnel had gouged a bloody trench across his leg moments before he'd been shot, and Sherlock smugly took the credit for providing at least 80% of the motivation for those changes. The regular sex certainly played a part, of course, even if Sherlock had found it a bit disruptive to his thought processes at first. It was an effort to keep focused on the bees instead of smoothing the thick, sleep-rumpled waves of John's dark auburn hair; because, given past experience, he knew it probably wouldn't stop there.

"So, okay, obvious, but I'm supposing that means you've proved Hendrick didn't actually die from an allergic reaction to the bee sting?" John finally hazarded. When Sherlock only lifted his finely-arched dark brows higher, letting a little of his inner amusement and approval show in the slight curl of his mouth, John sighed and gamely went further. "The only thing I can think of is if someone injected something at the site of the sting."

Giving John the smile he deserved, tilting his head in a relenting manner, Sherlock knew he must explain what would be next to impossible for John to come to on his own, even if he were as intelligent as Sherlock—though John was still nicely above average and more intuitive than Sherlock had once anticipated. Indicating the bee he had just settled onto the slide, its tiny legs waving very slowly in the air, Sherlock said, "This—and these—are some of Hendrick's bees. I've been testing them with varying hypotheses in mind, and I've found that they have been ingesting poisonous nectar and pollens. I will have to go back to the property to confirm my theory on how it was done."

"But, wouldn't that kill the bees, though?" John asked; gratifyingly not questioning Sherlock's conclusions.

Shaking his head, Sherlock loaded the pipette with the same diluted mixture of chemicals he'd used on the last bee. "Bees often gather pollen from poisonous plants," Sherlock said, repeating his procedure on the new bee. "Hendrick's brother in law, Peter Worthing, was clever. He knew Hendrick got stung fairly regularly, in spite of his years of apiological knowledge, and knew Hendrick frequently tasted the honey directly when harvesting from his hives." The liquid dribbled over the bee and pooled beneath it, going from a faintly cloudy pale yellow to an even cloudier pale green. "Some plants are poisonous to humans and most animals, but not insects. Or some birds, occasionally. Plants like oleander, nightshade or relatives like datura, just to name the first that come to mind."

"Ah, true," murmured John, his gaze moving past Sherlock and focusing on something that brought a little smile to his face. "Mrs. Hudson's coming over through the garden." John set his mug on the edge of the lab table and closed his robe, tying it in a loop knot by old habit before going toward the sliding glass door to the garden. Sherlock couldn't help a little smirk at John's oddly chivalrous manner around their landlady, or any woman, for that matter—certainly some of this particular behaviour was due to John's self-consciousness about his scars, but Sherlock had observed that it was just an addition to an existing modesty when in mixed-gender company—and it showed in John's language, as well, bringing him to use little to no profanity around 'ladies'. If it wouldn't get him a dirty look, Sherlock would've called it adorably atavistic, but he still sometimes thought it in the privacy of his own mind.

Sherlock looked over his shoulder to see their landlady approaching through the garden along the main path between the two houses. She was old enough to be mother to either of them, though aging rather gracefully. On the plump side of curvy, skin the deep warm brown of fertile earth, loosely curled short black hair streaked and specked with silver and white strands, Mrs. Martha Hudson stood barely an inch or two shorter than John, who was almost exactly six foot, just a few inches less than Sherlock—who, granted, was taller than most.

"How's the morning, boys?" Mrs. Hudson asked as John let her in, a bright smile bringing deep dimples to her slightly rounded cheeks. She had a light-hearted approach to life in general, and had apparently adopted her lodgers as surrogate sons, which started with match-making them from the moment Sherlock had brought John to see the place, and continued with feeding them up at every opportunity. "I went on a baking jag last night, so you'll have to help me with some pastries that need eating."

"I dunno, Mrs. H, that's going to be such a hard task," John teased her easily, taking the mostly opaque plastic container from her and prying up one corner to see what was inside. "Ooh, Sherlock, those berry tarts you like. Thanks, Mrs. Hudson," John said as he put one arm around her and kissed her cheek.

"Bring the container back when you're through," she replied, patting John's chest as he half-hugged her, and then gasped slightly and snapped her fingers. "I almost forgot! There was a phone call on the landline from someone asking after you, John."

Sherlock looked up from his damp, dopily unhappy bee to see John's expression go uncharacteristically neutral.

"Oh?" John queried, setting the pastry container on the table next to his mug. "Who was it?"

She looked upward, as many people did when remembering something. "Lieutenant William Murray." Her smile was a little impish, as she'd made no secret of her admiration for 'military men'.

Despite her humorous expression, John's whole face went through a quick series of reactions: Surprise, immense pleasure, unhappy realisation, and then settling into a put-on expression of polite pleasantness that was nothing like the real thing—at least to Sherlock's discerning gaze. "Yes, good old Bill Murray, one of my old army mates." John said, nodding belatedly. "Right. Did he leave a number?"

Mrs. Hudson nodded, her face almost shouting her curiosity, and gestured off in the direction of the slightly smaller house where she lived, across the garden and actually fronting Baker Street proper. "I'll text it to you straight away once I go back across, all right?"

"That's fine, Mrs. Hudson," John agreed, much more genuinely. "Did he say anything else?"

"Just that he got the address from your brother, but your brother didn't have your mobile number." Shaking her head, Mrs Hudson put a gentle hand to John's upper arm and patted several times. "You should give your brother your number, John."

Sighing, John showed a regretful face and used a regretful tone, but Sherlock didn't believe either of them. "Mrs. Hudson, my brother and I don't get on. Haven't since before I joined the army. But I sent him my address and number when I moved in here. Whether he kept the information or tossed it, I don't know, but that's all I can do."

"Oh, John," she murmured, squeezing his arm once and then touching her fingers to his cheek. It was apology, sympathy, and regret, all in two words and that gentle touch.

Putting his hand over Mrs. Hudson's, John nodded again and, finding no words adequate, he simply took her hand in his, putting a little kiss on the back of it in thanks before releasing her to reclaim his mug.

"I'll go across and send you the number, dear," Mrs. Hudson said after a moment.

John made a soft sound of acknowledgement as he opened up the pastry container one-handed and perused its contents, as if choosing which one to eat was some kind of difficult decision.

Mrs. Hudson patted Sherlock's shoulder as she passed, then tugged at the sleeve of his dressing gown to make him look at her. At his querulous expression, she raised her brows, exaggeratedly tilting her head at John.

When he frowned, she rolled her eyes and just gave him a not—exactly—gentle push, nearly toppling him off his stool. Ah, yes. An unhappy John would fall into the category of 'relationship maintenance' and should not be left to sort himself out alone; or so Sherlock had come to understand in the course of the last handful of months, which was confirmed by Mrs. Hudson's current vehemence.

"Enjoy the goodies, boys," Mrs. Hudson said with too-bright cheer as she all but scurried out and slid the glass door shut behind her. John didn't even look up.

Sherlock turned to John, still a bit uncertain how this comforting thing was supposed to work, let alone when it was appropriate or whether John would accept it at this time—sometimes he did want to deal with his issues by himself, but Sherlock was still working out the pattern. Giving himself a mental shake, he quickly transferred the bee back to the enclosure, cupping it in both gloved hands this time because it was almost fully recovered and not happy about having been restrained. He got it in without injury to himself or the bee and then turned back to John as he removed the gloves. "John?"

"Want one?" John asked, his tone a bit off and his eyes on the pastries instead of Sherlock, sliding the container closer to Sherlock.

Ignoring the poor attempt at distraction, Sherlock turned on the stool to fully face John, starting with, "You told me Bill Murray saved your life." Sherlock pressed his lips together for a moment, then just gave up and carried on as he wanted, rather than trying to figure out what he *ought* to say. "I would think you'd be happy to hear from him—and you were, if only briefly. What changed your first reaction?"

John's ears were going a bit pink and he looked away for a moment, putting his mug down before returning his gaze to Sherlock's, the false 'I'm fine, it's all fine' expression gone. "I am happy to hear from him, of course, but…we were really close friends, as I've told you…and…" John let out a short sigh and gestured vaguely at Sherlock and then himself. "He doesn't know I'm bisexual."

Just before the word, 'So?' could fly out of Sherlock's mouth, he held his lower lip between his teeth for a moment, and then said, "I wouldn't have thought you'd be close friends with someone who would be bothered by that."

Scrunching up his face in something like a mix of frustration and apprehension, John shrugged, coming around the edge of the table to stand closer to Sherlock as he replied, "I wouldn't either, but I never actually *said* anything and I…" John reached out and ran his forefinger down Sherlock's somewhat prominent Roman nose, briefly touching his curled forefinger to the end of Sherlock's stubborn pointed chin as he continued. "I don't want him to react poorly and disappoint me, while possibly hurting you," he finally admitted.

"What, because I'm gay, you fear he might somehow *blame* me for 'making you go gay'?" Sherlock supposed, not quite making the finger quotes physically, but indicating them pretty clearly with quirked eyebrows and a sassy tilting motion of his head. It almost made John smile, his lips twitching askew for a moment.

"Something like that, yeah," John confirmed, face and voice going sad again. "You are…you are everything to me, Sherlock," he said earnestly, going a small measure closer to run his fingers through Sherlock's sleek black hair and then cup the back of his neck. "I'm not ashamed of loving you or of being loved by you, but it's a different atmosphere in the military...though it is changing, I..." He shook his head, expending whatever else might've come at the end of that sentence in a sigh. "Look...my brother James is a homophobe and a drunkard, and I've heard some pretty ugly things come out of his mouth, but what there is of the rest of our relations would rather keep *him* in the family than me, just because he's straight. I didn't feel...right...bringing all that up with Mrs. Hudson, but...still...I loved Bill like the brother I wished I had, but if he turns out like James after hearing about you and me, then..." Again, he didn't finish his sentence and just shook his head, slowly leaning into Sherlock till his forehead was pressed against the lapel of Sherlock's dressing gown.

"You'd be, essentially, losing another brother," Sherlock surmised, nodding. John's head bobbed in agreement, his face still pressed against Sherlock's chest, letting out another sharp sigh. "I don't know enough about your Bill Murray to predict his actions, but if you were that close for years, I don't think you could have missed *some* indicator of homophobia if it was present."

"I don't know..." John took a deep breath and stood up straight, the hand at Sherlock's neck sliding down to his shoulder and staying there. Looking up at Sherlock as if hoping he could say something more to convince him his worries were unfounded, John didn't speak further.

"You've seemed unconcerned that our relationship is known to those we interact with regularly," Sherlock pointed out in reasonable tones. "Lestrade and others at the Yard—Gregson, Hopkins, and Jones; even the female officers, Hill and Forbes, and others—we've worked with all of them and you've never turned a hair. It's never been an issue before." He paused, but then added with certainty, "I'd have noticed."

Smiling a little, still a bit melancholy, John rubbed idly at Sherlock's shoulder as he said, "You would have, I know." Shaking his head, running his fingers down Sherlock's arm to take his hand and hold it firmly, thumb rubbing over one of Sherlock's knuckles, John made a self-deprecatory stab at another smile. "I'm probably overreacting, and I'll be okay. I think…maybe it's the fear of my former life coming into contact with my current life, as if my past might somehow ruin my present…maybe…I don't know, it's not logical, Sherlock."

"You cannot fear that anything this Lieutenant Murray might say or do would change my feelings about you, John," Sherlock said firmly, frowning a bit.

It was clear John was going to deny it, but then sighed and looked apologetic. "Maybe that's it, but not…not consciously. I think you might be right, though."

"Of course I'm right," Sherlock said without hesitation.

This time John did chuckle, if only softly and as if he was surprised by it. Bringing his other hand up to press Sherlock's between both of his own, John shook his head and held Sherlock's hand to his chest. The smooth skin there was warm and Sherlock could feel the steady beat of John's heart through the flesh and bone beneath. "Forgive me for being a bit daft for a little while?"

Rolling his eyes as if John was some sort of monumental thorn in his side, Sherlock shook his head, slipping his hand free to pull his friend and lover into his arms. "I could forgive you anything, John Watson, but there's nothing *to* forgive." Sherlock felt as much as heard John's murmur of Sherlock's name, and John's arms stealing around him to hold on tightly conveyed his gratitude more than adequately. However, in light of stopping this maudlin trend, Sherlock added diffidently, "Although, you could still apologise, if you feel you must, by giving me both of the berry tarts."

"Opportunist," accused John, his tone warmer and far closer to fond than stressed.

"Is that a yes?" Sherlock smiled into John's hair.

"You'll steal them anyway if I don't agree," countered John, but his tone wasn't at all serious. "Sure, sure." Pulling back, he looked much more himself and yet there was a hint of uncertainty as he asked, "I'll go ahead and phone Bill back, then; and, if he's able, I'd like to invite him over. That okay with you?"

"Don't be an idiot," grumbled Sherlock, bending his head to kiss John briefly. "Just let me know when and I can either make myself available or make myself scarce, whichever you require."

"Nope," John said with a shake of his head, though his smile was creeping back. "I require you here, always, and if Bill doesn't like it, then…well, too bad." He nodded as if that was that, decision made.

"Good man," approved Sherlock gently, kissing John again, only this time a bit more deeply.

"Mmm, yes. Yes you are," John murmured against Sherlock's lips before occupying them again for a good long while.

Two days later, John had not only phoned his friend Bill, but they'd agreed to meet for dinner. At John's deliberately casual mention that he was living with someone, it was Bill who'd insisted they both come, leaving John relieved and far more hopeful—Sherlock had been smug, unsurprisingly, apparently having more faith in John's choice of friends than John did.

In the meantime, Sherlock and John had gone to the victim's home to confirm or disprove Sherlock's theories about poisonous bees. They had found enough evidence—spaces in the victim's garden where flower pots had recently been removed, empty flower pots with plant remains, and, as final damning confirmation, a sticky residue that turned out to be concentrated plant toxin—to prove that Boris Hendrick had indeed been murdered. Pinpointing the killer was then a mere formality. Peter Worthing, Boris Hendrick's brother-in-law, had been charged with the murder, his wife Belinda apparently oblivious to her husband's greedy scheme to arrange for his wife to inherit her brother's wealth. As the handcuffs of Scotland Yard closed around the wrists of Peter Worthing, Sherlock and John shared a moment of triumph.

*

John recognised his friend almost at once when they paused at the entrance of the Fitzgerald, a not-too-rough, not-too-posh pub within easy walking distance of Baker Street.

Sherlock hung back, allowing John to make his way over to the booth and greet the man with a little measure of privacy; it was a good sign to Sherlock that Lieutenant William Murray brushed aside John's extended hand and hugged him heartily, Murray's rich laugh carrying easily across the pub's main room. A small smile curved Sherlock's lips as he watched the body language of his partner and his partner's old friend; the only negative he caught was John's nerves, though they were already less evident after that enthusiastic greeting.

Murray was built on a larger scale than John, though they were almost the same height, with a muscular build and large, strong hands. His face was a bit craggy and his nose looked as though it had been broken and poorly set at least once—no, twice—but it somehow didn't look terribly bad on him. He was bald, face also clean-shaven, and the overhead lights gleamed on skin the mellow golden-brown colour of old parchment. The slight epicanthic folds of his hazel eyes, along with a few other distinguishing characteristics, told Sherlock that John's friend, like John, was of mixed ethnicity; although John bore no East Asian ancestry, his father of Scottish heritage and his mother's people hailing from North Africa.

Parting from Murray, a happy smile upon his face, John looked around and beckoned Sherlock over impatiently, speaking as soon as he was in range. "This is Bill," he said unnecessarily, but Sherlock let it pass, holding out his hand. "Bill, this is Sherlock Holmes." Even as Murray's hand nearly enveloped Sherlock's, John cleared his throat briefly before adding, "My partner."

Sherlock felt Murray's hesitation, saw the surprised widening of his eyes, and watched closely as Murray looked from Sherlock to John, black eyebrows rising. He kept Sherlock's hand as he asked, "Partner?"

John nodded, and Sherlock was certain he would be watching his old friend for signs of disapproval, just as Sherlock was.

"Congratulations, John!" Murray said with every sign of sincerity before he grabbed John, yanking him into a hug again, and then reeled Sherlock in by the hand he still held, squashing him into the hug, as well. An involuntary grunt escaped Sherlock as the air was pushed out of his lungs, and a couple of his vertebrae popped. So much for John's ridiculous fears of homophobia, he thought smugly, but managed not to actually say aloud.

Within the hour they were in the middle of a meal, John and Murray babbling jovially, ranging from subject to subject without apparent plan, including Murray's losing track of John's contact information and subsequently having poor luck tracking him down again. The topic of Sherlock's work—and now John's— soon had Sherlock's cheeks burning from John's enthusiastic praise of Sherlock's talents, and of the work he did for New Scotland Yard, as well as private clients. Murray asked a great many questions, most of them intelligent and insightful; Sherlock could easily see how he and John had become friends. John admired intellect, even if it was still an unconscious tendency. Sherlock was also easily able to see that Murray was straight, though he clearly held John in high esteem and cared for him very much.

When John launched into their most recent case with the words, "Let me tell you about the time my partner got into bee bondage," Sherlock had already decided he approved of John's friend and brother-in-arms. He leaned back, a glass of surprisingly good wine in his hand, and listened while John told Murray about the Hendrick case, occasionally interjecting chemical analyses and the correct procedure around bees.

The case had been properly solved, Murray was suitably impressed and clearly happy for his friend, John was also happy on both fronts, and Sherlock had been allowed to keep the poison bees.

In all, a very satisfying conclusion.

The Stinger
By Stacey Albright

"What the flying fuck was that?" John Watson demanded, sinking into the plush seating of their private sleeper compartment.

"Murder on the Orient Express," Sherlock said mischievously.

"Mycroft, that bastard! I should have known. First class tickets...the Orient Express...all expenses paid... 'Oh, while you're there, would you mind apprehending "The Stinger of Segovia" who's hiding on the train?' John scowled. "Don't look at me like that. For all the cuddly black-and-yellow striped jumpers he wears the man's still an international assassin. You could've been killed!"

"I shouldn't say it..." Sherlock smiled and moved toward the Dom Pérignon resplendent in its silver ice bucket, "but it was thoughtful of him."

John was about to reply, but forgot what he was saying as Sherlock deliberately and provocatively popped the champagne cork, tiny bubbles spilling suggestively down the front of the bottle.

John had three thoughts then: firstly, that was wasteful; secondly, he'd never seen a bottle of champagne opened so filthily; and thirdly, how had he never known Sherlock could do that with a bottle?

"It's our honeymoon, you're not supposed to be engaging in anything dangerous or reckless. You promised," John continued as his lover moved toward him, two glasses in one hand.

"Oh, I don't know about that." Sherlock smiled, brushing wet lips across John's collarbone. "Permission to climb on board?"

Among the Wildflowers
By Elinor Gray

Sherlock Holmes interrupted my mid-morning doze with a gentle hand on my shoulder. "I say, Watson."

I passed a hand over my face and sat up straighter in my armchair. The sun was spilling across the knotted rug carpet that adorned our Sussex cottage hearth, and dust swam in the beam of light. "Yes, Holmes?"

He smiled at me, fond and amused. I reached up to take his hand in mine and smiled back. Nothing could be more pleasant than the sight of him upon awaking, though I used to have rather a different opinion of such a situation. But he had a different motive in those days.

"I, ah," he said, shaking himself, "wondered if you would care to join me for a long walk. The sky is as clear as glass, and I fancy a picnic."

"I should be delighted," said I, getting to my feet. "Is this a ploy to get me to make you a picnic?"

Holmes had the decency to look ashamed, but I only laughed and kissed him.

"I'll see what's in the ice box."

There was cold chicken and a bowl of blueberries from Mrs Turner, a wedge of cheddar cheese, some butter, and a jug of lemonade leftover from the day before. In the pantry I found half a loaf of bread and two tomatoes. As I was making two chicken, cheese, and tomato sandwiches, Holmes came in, already wearing his sennet hat, and poured the lemonade into a canteen. He also came up with a rather large slice of Victoria sponge, seemingly out of nowhere.

He caught my look of surprise. "It's a day old, I'm afraid," he said. "I got it in town yesterday and then couldn't bear to eat it without you."

"I was home in the evening," I protested.

"Well, yes, but I just remembered it now. Oh, don't give me that look, John," he said, smiling and putting the cake in a small tin, "you'll benefit from it, even if it is a touch stale."

"Anywhere in particular you wanted to go?" I asked as I packed the basket. "Just give me a minute to change my trousers and put on my boots."

Holmes' voice followed me through the little cottage. "Nowhere in particular," said he, "but we will want to find a quiet place for lunch where the wind does not make it impossible for us to eat. And take a hat, my dear; the sun is very strong."

*

We walked out into the bright mid-morning sun, Holmes with the basket over his arm, I with the blanket that usually lay across the back of the settee rolled up and tied into a bundle. The breeze was fresh, and as we reached the top of the hill beyond the garden it had strengthened into a strong blow that threatened to snatch our hats. The grass rippled with the force of it and it pushed at us as we walked, seeming to guide us across the rolling downs.

Holmes did, in fact, seem to have a destination in mind, and he pressed on, despite the wind. We went away from the nearby school—nearby in a Sussex sense, rather than a London sense—and walked along the cliff edge. The sea, hundreds of yards below us, crashed and rumbled unceasingly. I tempted fate, walking closer to the crumbling chalk, but Holmes' reproachful shout over the wind brought me back. He reached out and took my hand, and said, "If you fall to your death, Doctor, I'll be very put out."

146

"I should hope so," I said, lacing our fingers together.

At some point, though what it was that suggested to Holmes it was the right point I wasn't certain, we turned our backs on the sea and walked inland for a while. The wind gentled, the sun beat down on us, and we stomped through several empty livestock fields for good measure.

It had been almost an hour since we left the house by the time Holmes finally said, "Ah," with satisfaction, and pointed out our destination. Ahead of us was an uncut wood, thick and dense, and for perhaps half a mile before it lay a carpet of wildflowers. We reached the edge of that carpet, and I could see dozens of different kinds of little flowers: a kaleidoscope of natural beauty. Holmes waded into the flowers a few hundred yards, stopped, looked around, and nodded.

"Put the blanket here, John."

I unfurled the blanket and laid it down carefully. The low hum of bees could be heard all around us, and the last thing I wanted was to try and have lunch on top of a few dozen of them.

Holmes sat down, took off his boots, and began to unpack the lunch. He had also managed to stow away notebooks and two pens, which he laid aside. I stood, letting myself cool down before I joined him. I was short of breath and had broken a sweat, while Holmes looked entirely unconcerned by anything, as usual.

"Come on," Holmes said, patting the blanket beside him. "Plenty of room to lie down." At my annoyed look he said, "After lunch, for heaven's sake. You can have a nap while I count the bees."

"I knew you were up to something," I said, taking a seat and removing my boots as well. I wiggled my stockinged toes, feeling indulgent.

Holmes handed me a sandwich. "I want to see what wildflowers they prefer, so that I can plant them near to the house."

"You know you don't plant wildflowers."

"You can encourage them," Holmes said.

"Suit yourself," I said, and bit into my sandwich.

Holmes expounded on the wildflowers and the bees as we ate, and his goals for hives of his own. We had only lived at the cottage a few years, and already the garden was taking form. Holmes was its architect, whilst I was the executor. I was getting quite good at digging in the dirt, and enjoyed the pattern of weeding, planting, watering, pruning, and fiddling. We had talked about a vegetable garden to go alongside the flowers, but Holmes' hives came first.

Once we'd eaten our sandwiches, we shared the sponge cake and the lemonade between us. I kissed icing sugar off Holmes' lower lip, which made him laugh, but he pushed me gently away before I could initiate anything more amorous.

"The bees," he reminded me. "I am observing them."

I lay back on the blanket, propped my hat over my eyes, and folded my hands beneath my head. "Observe away," I said, perfectly content to nap in the sun. I listened to him pack up the basket again and felt him shifting around until he was sitting close beside me. I heard his pen scratching in his notebook. I reached out with one hand and found the plane of his back. He murmured something; I let my hand rest there, thumb moving slowly back and forth across the fabric of his shirt, feeling the bump of his spine beneath.

I didn't quite nap, but I drifted for a while, soothed by the wind in the grass and the low hum of the bees. Holmes beside me was a warm, solid presence, making only the occasional observation aloud. I was warm from head to foot. It was perhaps the most relaxing hour I have ever spent.

I felt Holmes shift on the blanket, and then he was draping himself along my side, his head resting on my folded arm and one ankle crossing over mine. I blinked at the underside of my hat, oriented myself, and lifted it to look at him. "Do your bees not amuse you anymore?"

"They always amuse me," he said, "but I find myself distracted."

"Well," said I, "do you propose an alternate form of amusement?"

Smiling, Holmes leaned over and kissed me, his lips warm and a little chapped. His hand found a resting place upon my waistcoat buttons. I tucked my arm underneath his, my palm against his spine, and kissed him in return. He gazed fondly down into my face, and bent to kiss me once more. I put pressure on his back, keeping him there, and the kiss lingered. Holmes' breath was soft against my cheek. His lips parted, and I touched them with the tip of my tongue. He replied with a brush of his tongue against mine. I sighed, opening my mouth, and Holmes made a soft noise in the back of his throat as he kissed me more deeply.

We were fully in the open, and though we had not seen another living soul all day, the knowledge of it thrilled me. I tightened my arm around Holmes, pressing him against my side, and brought my other hand up to cradle his face as we kissed. His cheek was smooth, shaved just that morning. I slid my fingers into his hair and rubbed my thumb around the helix of his ear. Holmes shivered, despite the warmth of the sun overhead. His body was long and firm, his chest against my ribs, his knees bumping my thigh, and I felt him rock his hips subtly against mine.

Holmes' hand left my waistcoat and slid up to my cheek, my jaw. He lifted my chin, tipping my head back, and gave himself more room to lick deep into my open mouth. The breath he shared with me was growing heavy, and against my little finger I could feel his pulse increasing. My eyes were closed by now, my senses taken up with the taste of his lips, the smell of his hair cream and soap complemented by the flowers around us, the sound of the wind in the grass, and the gentle possessiveness with which he held my face up to be kissed. I shifted my own hand down to his side, slipping underneath his jacket.

He broke the kiss and I opened my eyes. He was looking down at me with some surprise, but his eyes were dark with desire.

"Watson," said he, and stopped.

I raised an eyebrow. "Yes, Holmes?"

"This is a little out of the ordinary, isn't it?"

"Well," I said, rubbing up and down his flank, feeling the steady rise and fall of his ribs, "it is not our usual environs. Rather more exposed."

"I am… quite overwhelmed by how much I want you just now," he admitted. His cheeks had gone a charming shade of pink. His prick was a stiff line against my hip. I lifted my head and kissed his neck in answer. He let out a shuddering breath and bent so that I could reach him more easily. I kissed and nibbled at his throat above his collar, never so vigorously as to leave a mark, but he did not need any rough treatment of that sort. Holmes is incredibly, deliciously sensitive, and the gentle brush of my lips against his skin is enough to make him tremble. I thumbed his nipple through his shirt. Our embrace tightened, and his leg slipped over mine to press against my groin. I gripped his thigh and pulled it higher, grinding him against me quite deliberately.

"Oh," he gasped, fingers tightening in my hair, "John."

"Hmm," I agreed, coming up against the barrier of his shirt collar. I had to let go of his thigh to deal with it, but then I was opening the top buttons of his shirt and I had my mouth on his beautiful, prominent collarbones. There is a scar there I like to thank for being no more than a scar, and as I licked it Holmes squirmed.

"God, I love your mouth," he gasped.

I dug my teeth in to hear him whimper. My own arousal was heavy between my legs, and the pressure of his thigh was no more than a tease. I adjusted my grip on him, paused in giving attention to his clavicular notch, and hauled him bodily atop me. He yelped, scrambled, and managed to settle with his legs spread wide across my hips and his chin level with my mouth. He pushed up onto his elbows, grinning with delight down at me, so I lifted my head up to kiss him again.

"Mmm," he said, into my mouth, and wriggled so that our hips were more neatly aligned. His prick was a long ridge against mine, and I used both hands on his backside to press him down firmly against me. We stayed like that for a while, trading deep kisses, grinding slowly together. He was still wearing his hat, and it shaded us from the bright sun overhead.

I imagine I could have lain there forever, enjoying the weight of him atop me. I returned to kissing his neck and caressing his back underneath his jacket, plucking at his braces and sliding my hands down into the back of his trousers. He pressed his mouth to my temple, his fingers in my hair. But his squirming grew increasingly insistent, and after a while he pulled away again, pushing himself up on his hands and resting his weight more heavily on my hips. I ground up deliberately against him to watch his eyelashes flutter.

"Will you suck me?" he asked, bold as anything.

"Oh, yes," said I, and rolled him onto the blanket beside me. He flopped onto his back, sighing, and wrestled himself out of his jacket. I helped him—or more accurately, got in his way—as he opened his trousers. He let me take over, resting on his elbows, and I wormed my hand into the placket of his drawers.

His prick jumped at my touch, hot and stiff, and his tip was already wet. I drew him out reverently and paused for a moment to admire him like that: more dressed than undressed, missing only his jacket and shoes; flushing pink in the heat; his cock and bollocks protruding obscenely from his open trousers, heavy and full and begging to be swallowed. He pulled his knee up, tipping his hips towards me and I bent to kiss his clothed thigh. I had to shift down the blanket, putting myself more on a level with him. My feet stuck off the edge.

"Oh!" Holmes said. "I've just had a thought."

I glanced up, my hand still lightly encircling his prick. He took off his hat.

"What if you… what if you turn 'round, and put your feet up at this end, and then… well, then I can return the favour."

"You are a clever one, aren't you?" I said, adjusting myself accordingly. Oriented like that, we were head to foot, facing one another, and I could get my mouth on Holmes while he got his on me. His nimble fingers were at the buttons of my trousers, brushing against my straining cock. In a moment I was free, prick springing out to meet his palm, and I raised one knee and planted my foot on the blanket for balance. He touched me lightly, drawing my foreskin over the head of my prick and easing it back again. His fingers danced up and down my shaft and combed through my tightly-curled hair.

Holmes has greyed slowly, going rather bald instead, but my hair has been determinedly whitening ever since I passed forty-five. The phenomenon has occurred evenly all over my body, and I marvel that Holmes, the most observant man in the world, has not noticed that he is sleeping with a much older man than he used to.

He bent and kissed my belly, as if he could read my sudden and very minor change in mood, and waggled his narrow hips at me. His cock waved in the air, plainly ridiculous. I gripped it to make him stop, which was his aim, and slipped the head into my mouth.

I managed to catch him off guard with this manoeuvre somehow, and the noise of surprise he made was splendid. He was slick and briny on my tongue, and as I tasted him he leaked another drop of fluid in his excitement. The angle of this variety of congress was perfect, for it was simplicity itself to sink him deeper into my mouth. He breathed out hard, gripping my thigh, and followed suit.

Bliss: to fellate and be fellated by my sweet, eager, brilliant companion in the summer sunshine. I sucked him deep and then pulled back to lave attention upon his cock-head, rubbing my tongue around his glans and against his slit. Holding him steady around the base, I could feel his pulse between my fingers. Simultaneously, his clever mouth enveloped me, plunging down exactly as I liked. He tickled my bollocks, lifting them away from my body and pulling gently, sending pleasure rippling up and down my legs. I grunted and took him deep again, almost into my throat. He clutched at me, groaning, and the sound vibrated through me.

I changed my grip, reaching between his legs to cradle his thigh over my shoulder and get a handful of his backside. He bucked and whimpered, and all at once he was pulling away. He let me go and began to struggle out of his trousers.

"You'll sunburn your arse," I said, grinning.

"John, hop to," he replied, kicking his trousers off to the side, "I'm not interested in your humour right now. I want you as naked as possible, and I want it immediately."

He was still wearing his shirt and his socks, but I forgave him those. His prick stood up proudly from the thatch of hair at his groin, and his stones were full and heavy. I reached for him, mouth watering, but he stopped me with a hard hand on my shoulder.

"John."

"Oh, you--" I said, but I obeyed. I took off my socks, too.

"Now, on your back, my dear fellow," Holmes ordered, pushing me flat. He swung his leg over, knees on either side of my head, and his long prick hung quite obscenely in my face.

It was perfect. I could run my hands up and down his thighs, over his arse, and along his sides. I only needed to lift my head the littlest bit to lick his plummy tip. He groaned, bending over me, and took me back into his mouth. I pushed at his knees, spreading them, and he sank low enough that I could lie back and suck him without straining my neck.

He began to squirm again, rocking his hips, pushing himself in and out of my mouth. I encouraged it, squeezing his buttocks and dipping my fingers between his cheeks. A little friendly pressure against his arsehole and he was moaning around his own mouthful.

My own pleasure was secondary to bringing him his, but he began to apply himself to the task. He licked around my head for a while, teasing me, his nimble tongue working against my most sensitive flesh. Then he began to swallow me in increments, bobbing deeper each time. He kept his teeth carefully covered, and I could feel where his spit escaped his lips and slid down my shaft to slick his hand. He stroked me too, little twisting strokes that ratcheted up my pleasure. Soon his lips met his fist, and he was jerking me up into the pit of his hot mouth. My hips rose of their own volition, eager for more.

Sucking him affected me as profoundly as being sucked, and I could feel the pleasure gathering low in my gut. I spread my knees and rocked up into his mouth, even as I pulled him down into mine. My throat had opened, and with every rolling thrust he reached the back of it. I was close and he could tell: he increased his pace, his grip tightened, and he pulled my thighs open wide. I had to release him, pull away so that I could breathe, but I stroked him as I panted. He understood, bracing himself on the blanket, screwing his mouth down around me and setting himself to the task of bringing me to my peak.

It wouldn't take much. Already I was trembling, my hips lifting, my cock swelling. I was gasping and groaning into the soft flesh of his thigh, nipping him as gently as I could, and my climax built inside me. He sucked my head, tonguing my slit, and stroked me rapidly, with the ease of long practice.

I slapped his side in warning and he moaned in reply, and then my hips rose clear off the blanket as I reached my peak. I spilled, hot and heavy, pulsing, into his greedy mouth, and he sucked me down with relish. I groaned his name, reverent. He squeezed my thigh and let me down gently, sucking me clean and wiping his mouth with the back of his hand.

He was shaking, his cock red and dripping, his bollocks pulled up tight. He was near his own peak and deserved the release. His belly heaved; his thighs trembled under my hands. He groaned aloud when I licked him, pushing forward at once, plunging into my open mouth. I took him deep, barely having caught my own breath, and he rolled his forehead against my thigh, sobbing with relief. Two knuckles firm against the root of his cock behind his bollocks, and I felt him stiffen, his pelvic muscles pulled taut. The pitch of his voice changed as he cried out, "John!"

Then he was jerking in my mouth and I held onto his hip as I drank him down. He arched and panted, trapped, hips twitching. When he stilled, head hanging, his hair tickled the inside of my thigh. I swallowed and pulled away, throat thick, lips sticky. Holmes lifted his knee and collapsed to the side. We lay gasping at the wide blue sky. His hand found mine as he began to laugh.

We laughed like lovesick old fools, fingers knotted together, sprawled on the blanket in the grass. A bee landed on Holmes' bony knee. He was still wearing his bloody socks. I pushed myself to a seated position, and he did the same; his kiss was salty and familiar. He offered me the bottle of lemonade, and the taste of that after the taste of him was strange and sour. I grimaced; Holmes laughed and kissed me once more.

"You really will burn," I warned, as we lay down again, still top-to-tail, hands joined.

He sighed. "So be it, then."

I closed my eyes. "Someone could come by anytime."

"The shock would do them good," Holmes said.

But it was too hot to lie exposed in the sun for long: reluctantly, we put ourselves back together. Holmes left the top two buttons of his shirt undone so that his throat was exposed, and he threw me a knowing smirk as he did it. I tipped his chin up with my finger so that I could kiss him between his collarbones. He put his hat back on, and we tied up our boots, gathered up the blanket and basket, and set off across the field for home.

"A most satisfactory outing," he said, taking my hand as we walked.

"We should do it again."

He smiled, looking out across the downs towards the sea. "Perhaps," he said. "Although I fear you may be right about the burn."

The Honeycomb
By Lucy Jarsdell

As popular as it was, John Watson could not find it in himself to really like The Honeycomb. It wasn't the club's clientele which troubled him, though no doubt most of London wouldn't have shared that view. Nor was it the romantic and rather chaotic bohemian air of the place, fairly harmless despite John's personal distaste for it.

No, it was the décor. Looking around the main room, a modern dance music record playing too loudly in the background, he took in the large hexagonal print on the red and gold wallpaper, the matching pattern on the monochrome carpet, the gilded bees dangling from the light fittings, and the profusion of silk flowers spilling from every table and corner, and felt that, really, the motif had been carried too far. It was fashionable, but John's aesthetic was a few years behind the times; he had yet to catch up to the garish sensibilities of 1966.

Had it not been for his long and enduring friendship with the proprietor, he would never have set foot inside. But Evan was in trouble, and John could not fail a friend in need.

John had been in the club barely a minute—just long enough for the curiosity of the few early patrons to make him feel very out of place—when Evan's assistant, a young man who has only ever been introduced to John as 'Millie', rushed out from behind the bar and clasped his arm.

"I'm so glad you're here," Millie said breathlessly, "Mr Welles has been so worried about something, he won't even tell me what!"

Without further ado, John was ushered through a door behind the bar, down a narrow corridor, past several untidy storage rooms, and into Evan Welles' office.

The room was papered with photographs, some sensible posed ones from their army days, and some more recent ones in colour, showing Evan looking unnervingly middle aged and spectacular in his outlandish clothes, with similarly-garishly dressed crowds of friends. Evan himself sat at the desk, his portly body wrapped in a dark red smoking jacket, his thinning hair slicked over to one side, his face creased with uncharacteristic worry. Opposite him sat a tall, lean man in a sober suit, whom John didn't recognise. Evan rose to greet him affectionately, effusively, pressed his hand, asked him to sit, then turned to the stranger.

The stranger's attention was on John.

"You are bisexual," the stranger said in a deep, smooth voice, his eyes roaming distractedly over John. "You remained in the military after your National Service, until you sustained an injury which forced your retirement. You're content to remain 'under the radar', as it were, allowing others to assume you are heterosexual, though you ally yourself with homosexual men in your work. You are distant from your family for reasons separate to your sexuality, and cultivate close friendships. You met Evan while in the service and remain fond of him, despite misgivings about his club."

Having delivered this extraordinary monologue, the man took a languid pull on the cigarette he held, and receded into quiet, either oblivious or uncaring towards John's astonishment. Struggling to decide how much offence he should take, John looked to Evan, who gave him an apologetic smile.

"This is Sherlock Holmes, John," Evan explained, cringing slightly. "He's a detective. He, ah, he deduces things about people. I didn't tell him anything about you."

"No... no, I know you wouldn't," John replied. "But—"

"How? Why?" Holmes said. "To save time. I want the people that I work with to be aware of what I can do. What I must do, to perform my investigations properly. I observe and draw conclusions through deduction, that is all."

His gloomy demeanour lifted a tad as he spoke of his work, a certain gleam of enthusiasm in his pale eyes.

"John values his privacy very highly," Evan said to Holmes, pleadingly.

"Of course. As I have assured you several times, Mr Welles, I consider discretion to be among the highest of my priorities."

"What's that you said about people you work with?" John asked, frowning.

"That's what I wanted your help with, John," Evan said, and he reached across the table to lay his hand on John's. John noticed for the first time how drawn and pale he looked. "There's been some awful trouble," Evan's expressive face flinched, and John realised he was close to tears. "Somebody has been trying to blackmail my customers, John. It must be stopped!"

John felt his stomach drop. "What happened, Evan? Start from the beginning."

One could never expect a concise account of anything from Evan, but by the end of his near-tearful deposition, John had the necessary facts.

A number of regular customers had ceased coming to the club, and shortly afterwards Evan was approached

161

by one of his 'old faithfuls' with bad news. The man had received photographs of himself leaving The Honeycomb with another man, along with a demand for money to prevent the photos being leaked. Further questioning among the regulars of the club revealed that the blackmailer had contacted at least eight others in this manner, many of whom had felt forced to pay and had left the scene, and even the city. The blackmailer had apparently picked their targets carefully, as they had all been men with something to lose; family, social standing, careers, all put at risk.

"And that's where you come in, John. I know I can trust you."

"Trust me for what?" John said, reeling. "What can I do?"

"I've asked Mr Holmes to help put a stop to this, and he has a plan. He will pretend to be a patron of the club and—"

Evan cut himself off as Millie came in to put a tea tray on the desk, and began to speak again once he left.

"Mr Holmes will make himself a target for the blackmailer and work out who it is once the threat is made. You've seen how clever he is. I've no doubt he can do it. But Mr Holmes has no reputation in our circle."

"I need an appropriate man to step out with," Holmes summarised.

John hadn't heard anyone use the term 'step out' since his mother had died.

"And so you want me to pretend to be his lover?" John asked. "I'm not...I'm no actor, Evan. You know that I'm not good at—"

"Oh John, *please*!" Evan cried, face reddening. "I can't think of anyone else who would fit the bill. You're always so good when things get tense, you always have been, and you simply exude respectability. You practically reek of it!"

"So, I would be the target, rather than Mr Holmes?" John asked.

"Quite," Holmes replied. "Though obviously, once I have apprehended the blackmailer, I will ensure that any material compromising you is destroyed along with the rest."

"You're very confident," John said sharply, frowning at Holmes, who had so little to lose.

"I'm very capable," Holmes replied.

John looked at Evan, desperate and unhappy, still close to tears, his dream of twenty years souring around him. He looked at Holmes, so self-assured in his clinical detachment. He heard the sounds of the club becoming noisier, busier. So many men entering their sanctuary, where they could show their true colours without fear.

"All right," he said. "Let's discuss details."

*

Thursday was decided upon as the best night for their first date. The club was busier than most week nights, but not so crowded that the blackmailer, should he be present, would not be able to pick them out. A pleasant bustle, rather than the Friday night 'meat market', as Evan charmingly called it. Evan had reserved a quiet table for them and Holmes was already sitting there, studying a small notebook, when John arrived.

John steeled himself as he approached the table and, when Holmes greeted him, he leaned down and kissed his clean-shaven cheek. Holmes put his notebook into his pocket and waited until John was seated until he began to speak.

"I've yet to observe anyone taking a particular interest in us," he said, his expression soft enough that anyone observing them would have thought he was saying something romantic. "Mr Welles has ensured that the most gossipy staff are aware that we are a couple, meeting surreptitiously. You garnered some attention when you entered, though I'm not sure why."

John glanced around the room and noticed more than one familiar face. "Some of the men here are patients of mine. It's always awkward to see one's doctor in public."

"Ah, of course. The doctor being party to aspects of one's life that are kept under wraps even here, yes?"

"The privilege of my profession."

"Yes." Holmes sat back in his seat and eyed John with interest. "You do have certain privileges. Including that of choosing your patients."

"There is no reason not to treat homosexual men. They have as much a right to health care as anyone else. If another patient chooses to judge me based on my clientele, they can go to a lesser doctor."

"Lesser?"

"Yes. I am as capable in my field as you are in yours. I consider our..." he waved a hand at the gathering at large, "community, to be important. They are worth looking after."

"How so?" Holmes asked.

"They are determined not to pretend," John replied. "Fighters."

Holmes' eyes studied the room. "Fighters, yes," he said after a moment. "You've known a few of those, haven't you. How long did you remain in the military after your national service?"

"Four years," John replied. "Got out in the field a bit more, once I had the qualifications and the clearance. Front line medicine."

"Frightening," Holmes said, voice lullingly smooth. "And exciting, no?"

"Never the same day twice," John replied. He knew he was being somewhat evasive, but the slow small smile that Holmes showed him not only expressed some sort of approval, agreement maybe, but was also the first genuine-looking expression he had seen on the man's face.

To John's relief their conversation moved on naturally from that point. John's military history and medical training, Holmes' university life, both their experiences of life in London. Holmes had studied chemistry, so they discussed a recent piece of research into chemotherapy that had been documented in a journal they both subscribed to. John had served on the jury for a murder case the previous year, and they discussed the outcome, the evidence that had been nearly overlooked by the police.

They sat close as they spoke, leaning their heads together or touching one another's hands on the table top when any of the waiters came near. Their voices were hushed enough that nobody would be able to tell their conversation was not typical for a romantic evening out. John found the smile he had tried to maintain lingered on his face more easily as the hours passed.

At the end of the evening, they left the club together and walked side by side through the dark, quiet streets, to the large Georgian house in which John had a flat. He kissed Holmes' cheek again as they parted.

If anyone had taken their photograph, he hadn't noticed.

*

"Is there any particular reason why you are single?" Holmes asked.

It was an hour and a half into their second 'date,' and John had had a couple of drinks, so it took him a moment to decide that no, Holmes hadn't meant anything rude. It was merely his falsely artless way, to which John was gradually becoming used.

"I'm choosy, I suppose," John said. "And...what you said the other evening, about me being safe under the radar, that was true. But I don't want that when I'm in a relationship. If I'm with a woman, I will tell her that I swing both ways. If I'm with a man, I tell him the same, and I want him to let me be honest with others, where I can."

"You don't want to pretend?"

"Yes. I'm not about to run through the streets proclaiming love for my own sex," John said with a short, shallow laugh. "But I'm not going to pretend I'm with some woman, or lie to my friends, just to make life easier. I don't...I just want to be." He picked up his glass and drained it.

"Is that why you are single? Hard to find a complimentary attitude, and choosy besides. Can't be easy. Or perhaps you've stopped looking," Holmes continued. "Do you fear, perhaps, the 'Well of Loneliness'?"

John narrowed his eyes at Holmes, but still couldn't detect anything more than curiosity. "My last girlfriend left me because she thought I was going to lose control of my libido and cheat on her with a man. The whole matter is...it's rather a sore point."

"Ah," Holmes said gravely. "I see. I apologise."

A waiter came by with another drink for John, Evan having ensured they were well looked after on their little dates. John sipped slowly, idly watching the singer, who was singing 'These Boots Are Made For Walking'. He had little taste for these modern pop songs; they made him feel old.

"Try to control your face," Holmes half-whispered. "You look sad."

"Well...give me your hand, then," John replied.

A long, bony hand was proffered, and John gripped it. Holmes leaned his head in close and John followed suit, distantly satisfied with how intimate it must look.

"You've never cheated on a lover in your life," Holmes said with certainty, and he was not wrong.

When they set off for John's flat later that night, he took Holmes' arm, and they walked with their arms linked for most of the journey. Of course, they had to let go when other people crossed their path. It wouldn't do to catch a blackmailer at the cost of John being outed for real. Still though, it was worth it, to give the blackmailer plenty of opportunities to take suggestive photographs.

And, John could admit to himself, it felt good. To walk through his city arm in arm with another man, largely unafraid. For such an odd man, Holmes' company had quickly become comfortable.

And for such a thin man, he was surprisingly and pleasingly warm.

*

It was Tuesday, and John arrived for their date first, for once. A waiter showed him to their usual table and asked where his boyfriend was.

"He'll turn up in his own sweet time," John said cheerfully, rolling his eyes.

"My last one was like that," the waiter replied with a grin. "You should tell 'im that if he's late, you won't have any trouble finding other company!"

When Holmes arrived he smiled warmly and, this time, leaned in to John's kiss to his cheek rather than accepting it passively.

"Have you heard about Berkeley?" he asked as he sat. "Looks like he'll lose his seat in Parliament."

John frowned, recalling vividly the disappointment that had had him feeling low and a bit lost after he had read the previous afternoon's newspaper. "Yes, I read about it. Pity to lose a supporter like that. But then, Wolfenden stands. Somebody will take it up again sooner or later."

The waiter approached the table and John saw an opportunity to be overheard.

"Tired, Sherlock?" he asked, trying to sound affectionate.

Holmes picked it up right away. "It's been a long day," he replied as a drink was placed on the table before him. "I feel better for your company though, John. As always."

He took a sip of his drink, smiling at John over the edge of the glass, and John was suddenly struck by the gesture; flirtatious, but it lacked the slight self-consciousness that Holmes had thus far allowed to colour their 'romantic' interactions. It almost felt genuine. The idea was close to unnerving.

"May I ask a question of you that you asked of me, the last time we met?" John said, covering his unease.

"Which question in particular?"

"'Is there any particular reason why you are single?'" John asked, imitating Holmes' lofty tones.

Holmes gave a smirk, then leaned back in his seat, eyes darting for a few seconds. He didn't look uncomfortable exactly, but perhaps a little thrown. Just as John was considering withdrawing his question, Holmes rested his elbows on the table and steepled his fingers.

"I have never been anything but single," he said. "There is nothing to explain."

John was certainly surprised. He had met people who had no interest in sex, and he had met people who had no interest in love, but he had never expected that Holmes was so inclined.

"You've never felt attraction?" he asked. "Never felt a...a pull to anyone?"

Holmes shrugged. "There was once a woman. But nothing came of it."

"A woman? Just one?"

"Yes, just one. She was unique. Exceptional." He drained his glass, and they made careful small talk while the waiter brought them fresh drinks. Then, to John's surprise, Holmes took his hand and used it to draw him a little closer.

"I can see your mind working, John," he said, voice hushed. "You are contemplating my precise sexuality, yes?"

John shrugged. "I suppose so," he said. "You never struck me as one entirely uninterested. But is that what you   are?"

Holmes stared hard at the gilded bee dangling from

169

the light fitting above their table. His fingers twitched around John's hand as he considered. Finally, gaze still settled on the bee, he replied.

"I don't know. I don't rule out the possibility that I may at some point feel attraction. But it seems not to be an essential part of my nature."

He looked unsettled, and John felt an uncharacteristic urge to pry. "You don't sound sure of yourself," he said.

"I'm afraid I have little data on the topic, really. Remiss of me, but I've never spent much time around others. I don't have an intimate circle, or anything similar. Aside from a handful of pleasant acquaintances, I stand alone."

"Why?"

"I am unique," Holmes said after a moment's thought. "Or as near as makes no difference. Other people do not understand that I cannot be expected to fit their...their..."

"Expectations?" John offered.

"That will do," Holmes said, and sighed. He looked tired, all of a sudden, and John felt abruptly guilty. He stretched his hand out across the table and touched Holmes' knuckles lightly. Holmes jumped a little at the touch, then stared at John's fingers for a moment, before lifting his gaze to John's face and giving him a small smile.

"I'm not upset, John," he said quietly. "I don't feel that I've missed out on anything. It's only that, so many things come naturally to me that are a mystery to others. But the opposite is also true."

John nodded, dithered, then changed the subject.

Later that evening, they once again walked to John's home arm in arm. Holmes decided that he wanted to practice his hand at imitating a drunk, so most of the way he leaned heavily on John and made loud, odd comments about any landmark they passed. By the time they reached John's door, Holmes had broken character and they were laughing.

"We should appear to be kissing," Holmes hissed as they mounted the steps to the front door, and John nodded, glanced around the street to make certain the coast was clear, then drew Holmes into the doorway. He put his hands on Holmes' waist, and felt Holmes thin arms drape heavily around him. In the shadow of the doorway, behind the shelter of Holmes' upper arm where it lay across John's shoulder, their faces were close enough that they must have appeared to be kissing. Their noses touched, their lower lips brushed very slightly together, and John closed his eyes. Holmes' breath was warm and he smelled of tobacco.

John leaned in further, opened his mouth and—

No.

No, no, they were just pretending.

Mercifully, Holmes backed away from him, giving no sign of having noticed John's slip.

"We have yet to be photographed, but I'm confident we've been followed tonight," Holmes whispered. "Keep your eyes peeled."

John felt a flare of apprehension, which faded when he firmly reminded himself that this was blackmail, not battle.

"I shall see you on Thursday evening," Holmes said as he backed down the steps. John nodded and gave a wave, and Holmes made his way down the path and onto the street.

John stood there on the dark step for some time, his hand over his mouth.

*

Thursday arrived, and John made his way to the club with a sense of trepidation.

He had neither intended nor expected to feel attracted to Holmes, who wasn't really his type, and with whom he had to work besides. And yet here he was; he hadn't been able to stop thinking about him. It was nearly a comfort to know that nothing would happen, Holmes had as much as said so himself. All John had to do was get through a few more dates until Holmes pinned down the blackmailer. If the lazy cur ever got around to photographing them.

He ran into Holmes a little way down the street from The Honeycomb, and they walked down the narrow stairs into the club together, the bouncer greeting them with a nod.

Their usual table had been kept for them, and as soon as they sat, the waiter was there with their drinks. It felt alluringly comfortable, like they really were a couple of two weeks standing, excited and hopeful in their relationship, accepted and at home in this little patch of their community.

John knocked back his first drink too quickly. Holmes gave him a considering look, but said nothing.

John felt worried that he would be awkward, but though he perhaps spent too much time trying not to stare at Holmes' patrician face or his eloquent hands, any ungainliness seemed to go unnoticed. Fortunately, Holmes had evidently very much enjoyed a case he had been investigating since they'd last met, and he was eager to discuss it. A matter of a murder victim that appeared to have been a victim of gradual, long term poisoning in the months before he was deliberately hit with a car. Holmes was a poor storyteller, and John

172

struggled to keep up at several points, but there were a lot of medical details to the matter that he could draw out, and it became a gratifying conversation.

For the first time, a patient of John's approached them to ask how he'd been and if it was true that he was friends with Evan, and that seemed to open the floodgates for several others to politely interrupt them with questions and friendly chat. John began to wonder if, through Evan or his work, he had somehow formed a link to every gay man in London.

Holmes would join their conversations every so often, making observations or even clever little jokes, and John felt vaguely proud of him. If he'd really brought a man here as a date and he had behaved as Holmes...as *Sherlock* had, John would have liked him all the more for it. As it was...

Damn.

When the singer got up on the stage, they were left to themselves, and John took the opportunity to ask a question that had been troubling him.

"You're sure we haven't been photographed?"

Sherlock nodded. "Quite certain. Not even last night."

"But we've definitely been followed?"

"Yes." Sherlock leaned closer to John, his eyes on the singer. "I know what you are thinking; why follow us and not take a photograph, especially given the kiss. Even walking arm in arm would have been enough to cast doubt on us. And yet nothing. It's strange."

Once the singer had finished, they rose to leave, answering several goodbyes on their way to the door. They linked arms comfortably now, and John was glad of it despite the twinge of awkwardness he felt, as the night was distinctly chilly.

"You know," Sherlock said as they made their way through the dark streets, "I rather enjoy your company."

"Really?" John felt immensely flattered. "I thought you preferred to be on your own."

Sherlock shrugged. "I generally dislike the proximity of other people, and the way they interact. Always so false and reaching. You're different. And I don't find touching you unpleasant in the least."

"Well, that's just as well," John said cheerily. It was nice to know that, even though his attraction was unreciprocated, he had at least made a good impression. He was smiling by the time they reached his front door, and he tugged Sherlock into the doorway for a repeat of their previous performance.

This time however, to John's astonishment, when they came in for their well-screened fake kiss, their lips met. And it was Sherlock who had closed the gap.

John opened his eyes to find Sherlock staring at him, alert and confused. All good sense simply left him; he gathered Holmes closer and kissed him as firmly as he dared, leaving no room for doubt. Seconds passed, before Sherlock gasped and pulled away, and John's heart sank as he watched him stumble down the steps. But halfway to the pavement he stopped, gave a great, confused groan, and turned back to John with an expression of pleading.

John held out his arms, and Sherlock Holmes went to him.

*

He was inexperienced, of course, but John had experience enough for the both of them, and he knew how to be gentle. Sherlock had learned to kiss at some point, and did so very sweetly, but he couldn't work out

174

how to get John out of his clothes, or how and where he was permitted to touch. John showed him; showed him the knack of unfastening buttons that felt the wrong way round, guided his hands to spots where the skin was thin and the nerves lively, caressed and soothed him until he shivered.

They ended up in John's cosy bed, curled up together in the jumbled sheets. John had stripped Sherlock down to his undershirt, and tucked himself between those long, long legs, one hand stroking a trembling thigh and the other aiding his mouth as he sucked him. Sherlock keened and gasped and spluttered out fragments of words, and when he was done, he clutched John to him, clinging on to him as if for dear life.

John soothed him, kissed him, and when Sherlock's hands began to roam, he peeled off what remained of his own clothes and let him explore as he wished. Sherlock's approach to him was a charming mix of curiosity and satisfaction, as he no doubt tested what little he knew of the human body in arousal on John, and found delight in discovering his knowledge to be real, or to be easy to expand upon. After long minutes of sweetly giddy touching and testing, smiling like a ray of sunlight, Sherlock finally wrapped one of those long, bony hands tentatively around John's cock, and he wrapped his own hand over it, guided Sherlock, showed him what he enjoyed, and they both lay contentedly in the nest of sheets and watched with fascination the difference in the shapes of their fingers, the tone of their skin, as Sherlock's hand brought John to orgasm.

*

John was woken by a thump and a muffled curse. He reached out to switch on the light and discovered Sherlock crouched on the floor, having tripped on the rug in the dark. He was dressed but for his shoes and coat.

"It's four a.m.," John said, squinting at the clock. "Where are you going?"

"I must attend to matters of the case," Sherlock said. "I had a revelation regarding the curious incident of the photographer in the night."

"What? There was no incident. He never took a photograph."

"Precisely! Meet me at The Honeycomb, this evening, six o'clock," Sherlock demanded. He grabbed up his shoes and, as an afterthought, approached the bed and bent to put a careful kiss on John's brow. Then he was gone, clattering out of the bedroom, and out of the flat.

John thought about what he had said, but finally came to the conclusion that he would have to wait for Sherlock to explain his bizarre statement, and went back to sleep.

*

"John! Mister Holmes!" Evan cried happily, as they crossed the dazzling room towards him. The club was empty, half an hour to go until opening for the evening, and despite Millie's important attempts to convince them that his boss was too busy to see them, Evan had quickly come to them once he had heard Sherlock's low, clear voice from his office.

"I have the answer to the case," Sherlock said brusquely. "And I'm afraid you aren't going to like it."

Evan flinched, the colour draining from his lively face. John grasped his arm and led him to a bar stool, having an inkling that alcohol would soon be called for. Sherlock eyed Evan, then John, and then turned his gaze to look at the other man in the room.

"Millie," he said simply.

Millie's face reddened and his posture sagged, and that was all the evidence that John and Evan needed to realise that years of friendship and hard work together had been betrayed.

"No!" Evan cried, and Millie made an awkward start for the door, but John darted into his path and seized him by the arms. Millie aimed a kick at John's shin, but it only glanced off him, and a few testing squirms made it clear to Millie that John was not about to let up his grip. After a few moments of struggle, he gave in and stood staring bleakly at Sherlock and Evan.

"He had the perfect opportunity to identify and follow his victims," Sherlock explained coldly. "And was in an ideal position to see his efforts paid off."

Millie let out a sob and sagged against John's grip. Glancing to the door, and then to Sherlock's alert face, John let go of Millie's wrists, and he crumpled to the floor. "How...how on earth did you..." Evan sputtered.

"Simple. We were a perfect target. We were spotted. We were followed. But we were not photographed, because we were known to be part of a trap. And the only person who could have known is the man who was standing outside your office door when we agreed on our tactics."

"Good heavens," John breathed. "As simple as that."

Sherlock smiled coolly. "See to your friend, will you John? I will settle the matter of the blackmail." And with that, he pulled Millie ungently to his feet and marched him out of the door.

And that was that. John kept a close eye on Millie as Sherlock led him away, but he offered no resistance as far as John could see, pacified by failure. The door at the top of the stairs clicked shut behind them, and John crossed to the bar, took a bottle of brandy down from the shelves, and handed it to Evan, who swigged from it inelegantly.

"All this time," he said weakly, tears spilling from his eyes, and John could only murmur soothing nonsense and pat his friend's shoulders.

*

John was in the sitting room of Evan's flat, having put his friend to bed with a mild dose of tranquilliser. They had sat up talking together for some hours, Evan telling the story of how he and Millie had met, how he'd come to offer him the job, how he'd trusted him, told him so much, shared so many fun evenings at the club with him. Evan had asked over and over again; why? why? why? And John had not been able to answer, except to say that people are sometimes weak, and sometimes make terrible mistakes. It was now the early hours of the morning and, having heard no news from Sherlock, John was deciding whether or not he should stay. Evan might need him in the night, and he was wondering if he could comfortably sleep on the sofa, when the front door opened and Sherlock walked in.

"I got everything," he said, offering John a thick folder. "Photos, negatives, letters, even some of the cash."

John took the folder and almost opened it, before remembering how much damage the contents had done.

He put it down on Evan's writing desk. "He can decide how to handle it when he's calmer," he told Sherlock. "It'll do him good to have a part in settling the matter. Help him lay the whole nasty business to rest."

Sherlock nodded. He glanced awkwardly around the room, picked at his fingernail, scuffed his shoe against the carpet, then very determinedly looked John in the eye.

"I play the violin," he announced. "Well, but sometimes loudly. I prefer strong tobaccos and I eat only at irregular intervals. I suffer dark moods and am sometimes in a fug for days, though I generally make my way out again on my own."

John frowned at him. "Why are you telling me this?" he asked. "Are you trying to drive me off?"

"No! No." Sherlock stepped forward and awkwardly reached out to catch hold of John's hand. "I merely thought that we ought to know the worst of one another. Before we...embark on anything."

He was deeply endearing, that brilliant man looking so hopeful and out of his depth. He could have told John practically anything and he'd still have wanted him.

He took Sherlock's hands and led him to the sofa, kissed Sherlock gently, and told him all of his worst habits and most terrible mistakes. And Sherlock was still there with him when the sunrise woke them both.

Be Prepared
By Janet A-Nunn

Sherlock was worried. He knew when looking became snooping and he'd crossed that line seven minutes ago. Sitting amidst a pile of boxes and detritus in John's old room, clutching a bottle-green sweater to his chest, he stroked the tiny bee badge sewn onto its sleeve.

Words.

Buzzing around his head.

Young John. Boy Scout. Beekeeping badge. Uniform. John in shorts...

JOHN. IN. SHORTS.

The man himself stood leaning against the doorframe looking at six foot of gorgeous folded amongst the clutter. He stayed silent until Sherlock eventually came back to him.

There you are.

"Bees John?"

"Yeah. The Scout Master kept hives. Our troop helped look after them to earn our beekeeping badge."

Sherlock's face creased into a smile, he held out the sweater. "Your first uniform?"

"Yeah."

"Reminds me of that time you wore shorts last summer..."

"Yeah."

"I like you in shorts John."

"I remember, Kitten."

"If I went downstairs could you find those shorts and join me in fifteen minutes?"

"I think I could do that Sherlock."

*

Fifteen minutes later sees Sherlock with his hands shoved down the back of said shorts, a slender finger finding a slick passage. He draws back from their kiss.

"Lube John?"

"Be prepared Sherlock. Boy Scout motto."

Sherlock grinned, "I doubt he had this in mind."

"Who, Princess?"

"Robert Baden-Powell."

What's the Buzz?
By Meredith Spies

The thing about having a beard made of bees is that it is heavier than it looks.

Bees, individually, are so tiny and fuzzy and *airy* that you would not assume even a thousand of them together would weigh as much as a giggle. But, they are, John Watson would happily tell you, bloody heavy. And tickly. And *there are fucking bees oh my God, Sherlock, what the hell!*

John Watson stood still as...well, still as a man with approximately eleven thousand well-armed insects on his face, neck, and chest. Inside, though, deep in his breast, he was a howling hurricane of rage. Sherlock had buggered off.

Sherlock had buggered off and left him standing in the apiary of Featherstonehaugh House. Apparently, John reflected as one intrepid bee braved the slick of petroleum jelly Sherlock had assured him would keep the tiny little danger-flies off his lips, a corpse was far more interesting than one's best friend hosting an all-bee disco on his face. John knew that all he would have to do was reach up to untie the string holding the queen's box in place under his chin and the bees would follow wherever she went, but he faced two problems with this:

One, John had no idea how to get to the tiny knot now buried somewhere under the forward flank of Her Striped Majesty's Air Force, and two, what the hell was he going to do with her if he got the box untied? It felt too cruel to throw her, and he didn't want to anger her minions into a stinging swarm (the one sting he'd incurred so far was madly burning and itching on his collar bone, and that was enough, thanks). And part of

183

him—a part he would never admit to, even under duress (and, let's face it, a bee beard was pretty much subsection 'A' under *things which can be considered to be duress*)—wanted Sherlock to be happy, to praise him, and that twisting ribbon of feeling winding down his bones held him in place.

"John!"

"Oh, my God! Doctor Watson!"

John's eyes widened by way of greeting, then narrowed in unspoken threat. Sherlock's lips tightened as the local DC, who had trailed out to the apiary behind Sherlock, quaked in shock at the sight before her.

"John, hold still," Sherlock began.

John narrowed his gaze even further. *No, I think now is the time for me to do the cha-cha. Of course I'll stand still, you great berk,* he managed to convey with the intensity of his glare. Sherlock had the good grace to look abashed as he gently removed the queen's box from around John's neck and began the slow process of moving the bees.

"What I don't understand is *why* poor Doctor Watson had to do this," the DC muttered, looking as if she could certainly do with a few drinks and possibly one more after those.

"To prove the bees are docile when handled properly and aren't tiny murder-machines," Sherlock replied, settling the queen into her hive. Already, the bees were de-bearding and following their raison d'être back home, leaving John a shaking, itchy, nauseated, shell of a man torn between murder and fainting.

"Couldn't you have just Googled it?" the DC wondered aloud. She seemed impervious to Sherlock's offended glare. "I mean, a live demonstration, then forgetting poor Doctor Watson..."

184

Sherlock ignored her. Loudly.

John, in turn, ignored Sherlock, also loudly, and stalked past the DC and towards the long, gravel drive where the rental car waited.

The DC watched John go before shaking her head. "He could've said no. Huh. Well. The things we do for love, right?" She smiled, but the expression didn't reach her eyes. "I'll be in touch, Mister Holmes, should any more questions arise over Mrs. Featherstonehaugh's murder."

Sherlock nodded once, briskly, his mind already on something else.

*

"DC Campbell seems to think you love me."

John flipped to the next page in his book.

"Did you hear me?"

"Mmmmhmm. I'm ignoring you."

"Why would she think that?"

Flip.

"John."

Flip

"John, why would she think—"

"Oh, for crying out loud, Sherlock! I let you cover me in bees! I don't care how good a friend a bloke is, you don't let them cover you in bees unless..." He dropped his book and pinched the bridge of his nose. "My life used to be normal."

"Do you miss it?"

John laughed. "No." He opened his eyes to find Sherlock crouched before him, face level with his own, closer than polite. "Sherlock..."

"Was she right?"

"DC Campbell?"

185

"John?"

"Ugh. Fine. Yes. Yes, I love you." John swallowed down the panic-giggle bubbling in his chest and tipped his chin to stare Sherlock down like a rabid dog if he had to. "I'm not exactly subtle about it, you know. Lestrade twigged to it a year ago."

Sherlock rocked back, his turn to blush and look away. "I am a fool."

"Finally, something we can agree on," John sighed. "So brilliant but so—" His words were swallowed by the sudden, hard, inelegant kiss Sherlock pressed to his mouth. John winced as his teeth cut into the back of his lip and his head tipped at an awkward angle, but the pain was fleeting. Sherlock shifted, slowly rising to his feet, pulling John along with him until they both stood in the afternoon-bright parlour, kiss softening, hands clenching at ribs and arms.

"Do you?" Sherlock asked, breath fast and rough, close enough so his words buzzed John's lips.

"Do you think I'd let just any man cover me in bees?" He chased Sherlock's kiss with his own, tea-flavored and sweet. "Do you think just anyone could make me as angry and scared and happy and definitely-not-bored as you?"

Sherlock pressed his forehead to John's. It was a lot of information, a confirmation of things he had been turning in his mind for years, curiosities sated. The flutter of it in his brain itched. "Why?"

"Does it matter?" John's fingers found Sherlock's. "Do you need an answer to every mystery?"

"Well...yes."

John laughed, falling back to his chair and pulling Sherlock down with him. "I suppose we can solve this one together, hmmm?"

"Like always."

"Always."

Summer
By Hallie Deighton

Hot summer sun filters through dappled leaves as Sherlock Holmes watches a bee dance over a bright yellow dandelion, focused on its own labours, ignorant and uncaring of the conversation going on over its head.

"Don't listen to Father," Victor Trevor says with an aggravated sigh. "I want you here."

Sherlock feels blunt fingertips nudge against his, somehow sharper than the dull spike of the blades of grass. Sherlock can't help it, he keeps turning the puzzle of Justice of the Peace Trevor over and over in his mind, as if the man's life were an algebraic or chemical equation. Observation one plus observation two means X equals...X equals what? There's something missing, a variable Y, that Sherlock doesn't have enough detail to answer. He's not even certain about the question, but once he makes the right observation he'll know what he's missing.

Except, Sherlock isn't sure he should keep observing. He has the disconcerting sensation that should he discover variable Y and answer question X, the fragile and unbearably precious friendship he has developed with Victor will shatter beyond repair.

Old Trevor watches him suspiciously now, barely speaks during their meals, except to exchange the lightest of pleasantries. Sherlock is not so unfeeling as to be unaware that Victor's father wishes him gone.

Sherlock is lost in the conundrum. To go now and keep his friendship with Victor, as it is now, or to stay...to stay and lie here in the shade with Victor's fingers touching his and perhaps... He's not sure what

189

he hopes for, but he is loath to leave…to never know what this other, more enticing variable will reveal.

"It's only that you gave the old fellow such a turn," says Victor. "He'll never be sure again of what you know and what you don't know."

Victor's dog, the architect of their friendship, lies on the other side of Victor, panting. Sherlock would forgive him a thousand bites for that alone.

"I don't want to know," Sherlock says quietly. Not if it means losing Victor. He'll turn off his thoughts, ignore, switch off his endlessly inquiring mind. He'll hunt and fish and swim and play cricket and simply be, just for the summer, if it means Victor will creep his hand into Sherlock's one more time as they pass the hedgerows.

"Well, I don't want you to go," says Victor sitting up, an obstinate look upon his handsome face. It makes him look much younger than his twenty years. It's a look Sherlock knows well. It's the look that says 'No, I shall visit you and talk to you, despite you being an utter prig'. It's the look that says 'You must come to stay over the summer, I absolutely insist, Holmes'. It's a look that makes Sherlock's heart beat more rapidly in his chest and a thousand chemical reactions spark within his blood.

Victor rubs the pads of his fingers over Sherlock's nails and Sherlock wonders if there will be an impression left afterwards, the faintest evidence of Victor's touch.

"Holmes…"

Sherlock looks up, can't do anything *but* look up.

Victor quirks a smile. "I want you to stay. Now, stop thinking about Father, do, and let me kiss you."

Sherlock thinks he's misheard for a minute but then as he looks up at Victor's face, at the way his blue eyes darken and fix on his face, he is as certain as he is of the type of ears that mark a boxing man that Victor is most certainly not in jest. That he hasn't misheard. His stomach flips in a way he's felt a dozen and one times since meeting Victor Trevor.

"You are serious," he breathes, his throat strangely thick. If he is truly the reasoning and observing machine he thinks himself, then his heart is pounding in such a way that he is afraid that machine's engine will shake itself to pieces.

Victor's gaze dips to Sherlock's lips, drawing with it a world of possibility.

"Of course I am, old fellow! Surely you don't think I'd tease you about such a thing…" His gaze darts back to Sherlock's face, a quizzical look forming on his brow. His handsome visage pales. "My God, Holmes…I thought we had an understanding…that we were alike, the two of us—" He shifts back a little, swallowing, runs his hand through his hair. "God, I've misunderstood—you must forget I said anything—"

Sherlock sits up quickly and grasps Victor's hands, stills them.

"I do… That is…I want to let you," Sherlock says and knows he sounds exactly like every imbecile he's ever had the displeasure to speak with, but the smile that blooms across Victor's face is worth it and Sherlock cannot bear it any longer. He kisses him, he does, and Victor's smile against his lips is incongruously brighter than the summer sun.

*

191

"Holmes!"

Sherlock Holmes is shaken from his reverie, watching the bee dance on the dandelion beside him, different dandelion, different bee, the autumn sun shifting down through the different leaves of a different tree, in a different time. Colder, the sun thinner. Across another lawn comes another man. Older, more portly, less hale, less hearty but dearer, *far* dearer all the same. Sentimental foolishness, but true nonetheless, as far as any emotion removed from cold reason could indeed be considered truth.

"I'm here, Watson," Sherlock calls, stretching out on the lawn and John Watson reaches him, slowly, but getting there in his own time, as he always does. He laughs and sits down beside Sherlock on the grass.

"Woolgathering, Holmes?" John asks. There's a hint of that same obstinacy in his expression that Sherlock saw in Victor's so many years ago, but different, mature and forged in authority and experience. Come to chase Sherlock in for his tea no doubt, and determined to do it.

"Studying the communication methods of bees, if you must know," Sherlock says loftily, indicating the heedless bee.

"Oh, of course," says John, not believing a word of it, Sherlock can see.

"I was thinking of an old acquaintance, an old friend," he admits.

"Oh?" John asks, but does not press and Sherlock thinks he might tell John tonight, over port, before the fire, safely couched in the guise of a mystery. He's surprised by how sharply the sting of that particular loss still lingers.

Yet… Perhaps… If he had not deduced Old Mr Trevor. If Old Trevor had not set him on the path to his unusual profession…. If Victor had not blamed Sherlock for his father's death… Then his path may never have led to Dr John Watson and a friendship worth more to Sherlock than life itself.

"Watson, my dear," says Sherlock. "John."

"Hm?" John says, and his eyes crinkle with humour as they often do when John looks at him.

"Come here, do, and let me kiss you."

John gives a startled laugh but his eyes darken and he does come, and Sherlock does kiss him, and against all logic, it feels to Sherlock as if it is summer again.

Love Song to a Bee
By Narrelle M Harris

When I was a boy I fell in love.
A bee in our country garden
mistook me for a flower
and kissed my skin.

I followed it home to the hive, and found that
other bees did not love me.
But my first great love was born —
the mystery of bees.
Their soft-striped bodies dusted pollen-gold
Their dances, more graceful
and more useful than English words.
Their honey,
sweetness the least of its wonders.
The greater fascination being its power to preserve,
to heal, to persevere,
fit for purpose after years
fit to kiss my tongue
through season after season after turning season.
And oh, the sting in their tail, a weapon
tiny and mighty, a defence
as cruel to the bee as to me.

My love of the mystery of the bee led to
my second great love,
The unraveling of the puzzle.
The wish and the will to know
and make known.
To lift the lid and understand the hive,

To understand humanity, from whom,
like the bees,
I seemed apart.

And then you came.
Soft and pollen-gold,
a preserver, a healer,
wounded by the weapon you had wielded.
So simple at first glance, but underneath
underneath oh! the *colony* in you
The many Johns you are,
With your healing hands that also fight,
Your great deeds of which you never speak,
With your pen that says more than your tongue.

Your language is as complex as the bees',
a dance of looks and deeds.

But the bees knew your name before I met you.
With their long and lazy *zhzhzhzhzhzh* and
their warm and embracing *oooooooooooooo* and
the syllable of satisfaction *hnhnhnhnhnhn*
(the sound I exhale in the second after our pleasure and
you lie between my thighs and kiss my chest and tell me
I am
the only one for you, now and ever).

You came to my lonely home and
mistook me for a man who could love and you
kissed me.
And you stayed.

And you showed me a puzzle.
The man who did not love was in love.

With bees, with mysteries.
With you.
The man who loved bees found a
queen around whom to build his home,
only to find his queen
mistook himself for a worker, and built his home
around me.

Zhzhzhoooooohnhnhn
John.

You are worker and drone and queen,
You are honey (sweet, healing, steadfast)
And you are the sting.
You are home and hive.
You are everything.
    All my loves in one.
    Bees. Mystery.
And John.

The Love of Apiology
By Amy L Webb

The Diary of John H Watson
15 June 1912

And so he is gone. Right up until the last moment I hoped for a reprieve, but it was not to be so. England has need of aid and Sherlock Holmes has answered her call.

Phrased in such a manner, it seems the only right thing to do and yet I cannot fully smother the bitter voice inside me that wishes someone else could have gone in his place. Has Holmes not done enough for this country? Hasn't he earned his retirement, fourfold over? But instead of relaxing in his cottage with all his many books, the man who loves him, and, of course, those infernal bees, he has gone off for what may well be years.

Holmes attempted to play down the circumstances under which he would operate but I am not naïve. I know the lengths one must go to in order to build the character he intends to take on whilst in America, and the associated dangers, and once he has done that, he still must infiltrate the spy network he intends to bring down. If he is identified as an imposter while doing so, it will mean certain death for him.

I am being selfish. If things are going to turn as bad as Holmes and his brother fear, we shall all be needed by our country in time and we will all face dangers. His mission is of vital importance in lessening those dangers and verifying that England is as prepared as she can be for the times ahead.

Knowing that does not make bearing his absence easier. In some ways, the hardest thing is not the danger, but the awareness that I cannot go with him and share in it.

He would not even let me go to the train station with him. He said it was to save my leg an unnecessary journey but I suspect it was really because he wished to say goodbye to me within the privacy of our home. Even if the emotions between us did not require a veil of secrecy, he is not a man who willingly expresses emotion in public, or even in private, unless under very particular circumstances.

I am more sentimental. More than he'd like, although he would never say such a thing; his occasional twitches of discomfort are eloquent enough.

My intention was to keep from discomforting him by merely patting his shoulder and wishing him well, but I'm afraid I wasn't able to restrain myself. My hand clutched his sleeve as if incapable of letting go.

"Please do take care of yourself," I said, fighting to keep the surge of emotion from my voice.

Holmes did not shake me off as I would have expected. Instead, he gripped my elbow and nodded. "As should you, dear fellow. England will not be worth returning to without you in it."

There was a fervent tone to his voice that I have only heard when he has lost some of his usual iron control over his feelings, an occurrence so rare that I am able to count each occasion on my fingers and have some left over. I think it was that moment when I realised just how long he was to be away.

I had too many words in my throat for me to be able to speak any of them so I settled for turning our contact into a true embrace, holding Holmes as if I could keep him with me just with my grip. He settled his arms around me in return, pressing his face close to my hair.

We stayed like that for longer than I would have expected him to allow. Eventually, he cleared his throat and pulled away, gathering up his luggage. He gave me a nod and turned to go out the door before tossing the final nail in my misery over his shoulder.

"Do remember to take care of the bees as well as yourself, Watson."

Blast those bees.

*

Daily Hive Checklist
Hive 2, 21 June

Observe bees at hive entrance. Having done so for the sixth morning in a row, I found myself still at a loss as to what I should be observing about them. There were some going in and some going out, and some apparently content merely to mill about doing nothing.

Do you see eggs? Today I think I successfully identified what an egg should look like. I felt a distinct surge of pride. Perhaps tomorrow I will be able to ascertain what it is I should be checking for when looking at them.

Can you find the queen? This one still eludes me. I find it all the more frustrating as I can remember Holmes showing me the queen of his first hive, not long after his purchase of it, and explaining how he identified her. My memory of the event, sadly, is largely of the sun shining down on his sleek hair and the way he had rolled his sleeves up to expose his wrists.

Is the brood pattern compact and plentiful? What is the appearance of the brood cappings? This point might as well be in a foreign language. I attempted to read an article in one of Holmes' journals that seemed to be about the subject last night, but it only left me more confused on the matter.

Evaluate your queen's egg-laying ability. (Do you need a new queen?) Having yet to find the lady in question, I shall have to continue to leave this point to be puzzled over at another time.

Inspect the larvae. How do they look? The larvae look, as always, like a cross between tiny maggots and the tapioca pudding my school used to serve. I presume that this is acceptable.

Check for swarm cells. (If necessary, take swarm prevention measures.) My word, I hope such a thing is never needed, as I shall have no hope of being about to tell that it is, and even less of knowing what such measures might entail.

Do the bees have food? If they do not, that is their own fault. There is a whole countryside of blooming flowers around them.

Clean off propolis and burr comb. I have finally found a chapter in one of Holmes' books that explained propolis but it did not give directions on what manner of cleaning it might require. I scratched off a few rough looking patches of what may well have been the substance with my thumb and hoped that would do.

Check hive ventilation. (Adjust based on weather conditions.) Adjust how? Holmes, how you expect me to be able to follow these instructions without rather more information is a mystery to me. Surely, with all your great brain power, you must have noticed that I paid very little attention to your hives over the years. I have no idea what I am doing, why would you leave me with this responsibility? Come back and do it your own damn self!

*

Post Office Telegram
3 July 1912
From: M Holmes, London
To: J Watson, Fulworth
BEEN ADVISED THAT OUR ACQUAINTANCE HAS ARRIVED WITHOUT INCIDENT INSISTED I UPDATE YOU BEFORE HE LEFT BEST WISHES FOR YOUR HEALTH

Post Office Telegram
4 July 1912
From: J Watson, Fulworth
To: M Holmes, London
TELEGRAM RECEIVED WITH THANKS AM IN GOOD HEALTH OTHER THAN BEE STINGS

Post Office Telegram
4 July 1912
From: M Holmes, London
To: J Watson, Fulworth
BEST REMEDY FOR STINGS IS AVOIDING BEES

Post Office Telegram
5 July 1912
From: J Watson, Fulworth
To: M Holmes, London
AM WELL AWARE TEMPTED TO ROLL HIVES OFF CONVENIENT CLIFF

Post Office Telegram
6 July 1912
From: M Holmes, London
To: J Watson, Fulworth
SUSPECT RESULTING RETRIBUTION WOULD BE
WORSE THAN STINGS KNOW S WOULD PREFER
ALL PARTS OF HIS HOME TO BE AS HE LEFT IT

Fulworth, Sussex
28 August 1912

Dear Mr Stewart,

I have been given your name by a mutual acquaintance, Harold Stackhurst, as someone in my local area who has a great knowledge and experience with the art of apiology. My name is John Watson and I am in need of your assistance.

I have been left with the care of five hives in the prolonged absence of a friend and am finding myself to be ill-prepared for the responsibility. My friend left me with copious notes and more than a few volumes but they were all written with the assumption that my knowledge of the subject is far deeper than it is. I must confess that I haven't paid quite as much attention to my friend's discussions about his hives as perhaps I should have.

I would account it a great service if you would allow me to correspond with you and ask for advice on a few points. I await your response.

Yours sincerely,
J H Watson

*

The Diary of John H Watson
8 June 1913

Today I think I have finally achieved a success in the field of bee-keeping, after nearly a year of looking after the creatures. I am not counting last year's honey harvest, largely because Holmes was still around at the beginning of the season and had a hand in creating it, but also because of the appallingly botched job I did of gathering it.

However, one of the hives swarmed today and I was able to successfully deal with the situation with a minimum of fuss and only two desperate attempts to find relevant information in Holmes' piles of notes. I will admit to rather stronger language than I usually employ but I feel the situation called for it. Persuading a large group of flying insects to enter a new home without getting more stings than I am accustomed to is not the easiest of practices.

The advice from Stewart was invaluable. I will have to send him a note of thanks. Without his advice on what to check for, I would have had no idea the bees intended to swarm and would not have had an empty hive ready to move them into.

Holmes had better appreciate all this when he gets back. If I had known that I would end up looking after the wretched things I would never have allowed him to get them in the first place.

That's not true. I would have let him keep a rabid bear if it would have kept him entertained and prevented the descent into a black mood that I feared would be the inevitable result of our retirement. I did not realise then how well he would be able to content himself with our quiet life here.

Our quiet life here is very, very quiet without him. I wish I were able to tell him all about today and hear his praise and amusement at my achievement.

He will come back eventually and things will be as they were before. The chair opposite mine will be occupied, our bed will no longer seem cold and empty, and someone else will be looking after these damned bees.

Fratton, Portsmouth
2 July 1913

Jack,

Just a quick note to say I'm back in the country. I've settled in Portsmouth for now but I'll be over your way on the 19th, if you'll meet me at our old watering hole.

Altamont

*

Post Office Telegram
23 July 1913
From: M Holmes, London
To: J Watson, Fulworth
RECEIVED REPORT OF YOUR RECKLESS ACTIVITIES MONDAY DO NOT EXPECT TO HEAR OF YOU ENDANGERING HIM THAT WAY AGAIN

Post Office Telegram
24 July 1913
From: J Watson, Fulworth
To: M Holmes, London
ADULTS ARE ENTITLED TO MAKE THEIR OWN MISTAKES

The Diary of John H Watson
7 October, 1913

I miss Holmes more now that he is only a few miles down the coast than I did when the Atlantic Ocean separated us. Our clandestine meeting when he first arrived only whetted my appetite. A snatched hour spent in the small cave closest to the tidal pool we used to swim in every morning is nothing compared to the long hours I wish to spend with him.

It is an interesting conflict that while my mind fully comprehends that more than one such meeting would be risking his discovery, and that possibly even that one was unnecessarily dangerous, my heart finds it incomprehensible that I do not visit him at least once a week.

I spent longer than usual at the hives today. When I am by them, surrounded by bees, he feels closer to me. Perhaps it is the hum of the bees filling the space in my life where he should be. Perhaps it is that the slow process of learning how to deal with them without being stung reminds me of the early years of living with Holmes, back when we were first trying to understand each other.

This winter is already colder than the last. I wonder if I should be making additional preparations to help the bees through it. Perhaps I should go through Holmes' notes to see if he has any information that might be relevant.

Fulworth, Sussex
29 October 1913

Dear Mr Holmes,

I am aware that your brother used to send you several jars of his finest honey every year at this time. In his absence, and given my custodianship of his bees, I thought I would offer you the same. I cannot pretend that the quality is anything close to what he would have been able to achieve but I am rather pleased with it all the same. I hope you enjoy it.

The bees and I are on rather better terms than we initially were. I certainly spend less time tending stings than I did. When I first tasted the honey from the hives, knowing that it was produced while they were under my care, I felt a surge of pride and some measure of affection for them. Perhaps it is merely the sense of teamwork, that both I and the bees had worked hard towards the creation of the substance, but I would swear it tasted sweeter than any purchased honey I have had.

All that being said, I will still be extremely relieved when Holmes returns and I can turn their care back over to him.

Kind Regards,
J Watson

Fulworth, Sussex
19th March 1914

Dear Mr Stewart,

I write to you with more urgency than is usual between us. I fear one of my colonies is in great danger and I would be extremely grateful if you would assist me.

This particularly colony did not weather the winter as well as the others but I had hoped that once the spring began in earnest, as it has over the last few days, it would begin to rebuild its strength.

If anything, the opposite has happened. I checked it this morning to find that the hive's stores of honey have been greatly diminished and the bees themselves are wandering the empty combs with almost a disconsolate air.

The situation seems so grave to me that I think it might be best if you came yourself to inspect the matter. At any rate, it seems strange that we have corresponded for so long without meeting. It would be of great service to me if you would come to lunch here, either tomorrow or Saturday.

I would be extremely grateful if you could reply by return of post, either with your acceptance or with further advice on the matter.

Yours sincerely,

J H Watson

Inside a copy of The Hound of the Baskervilles:

Dear Mr Stewart,

In much appreciation for all your help and advice on apiological matters and in memory of a joint mission to foil a burglary that was quite as exciting as anything detailed between these pages.

Yours sincerely,

J. Watson

*

The Diary of John H Watson
21st March 1914

If I had known that bees were so willing to commit burglary against one another, I think Holmes' announcement that he was intending to keep them would have come as far less of a surprise.

Stewart and I have moved the beleaguered hive to the cellar where their oppressors will not find them. He assures me it will be fine as long as I feed the bees there and move them out again after a few days. He has also shown me how to block the entrance so that only one or two bees may enter or leave at the same time, which he says will greatly diminish the risk of bees from other colonies entering and making off with their assets.

I have made careful notes on the whole matter which make far more sense to me than those Holmes left behind. I am not sure if he intends to write in code or if it is merely an unfortunate side-effect of the way his great brain works, but even with the knowledge I have after nearly two years of bee-keeping practice, I still find large chunks of them incomprehensible.

Of course, after over thirty years of knowing the man, I still find Homes himself often incomprehensible, so perhaps that should come as no surprise.

Listening to Stewart speaking about his love of apiology over lunch put me in mind of Holmes so strongly I felt a particularly powerful surge of the ever-constant pain of missing him. I think I finally realise just what it is he loves about his bees so much. There are so many facets and intriguing details about the study that an outsider cannot appreciate.

I suppose that means I am no longer an outsider but a true apiologist, albeit not a particularly gifted one.

Perhaps after a few more years, I will no longer need to send desperate letters to Stewart begging for assistance.

Hawthorn Cottage,
East Dean
24 March 1914

Dear Watson,

I am writing to thank you for the excellent lunch you provided for me on Saturday, not to mention the entertainment and, of course, the signed copy of *The Hound of the Baskervilles*. I have enclosed a copy of my own book, *Enemies of the Honey-Bee*, which I suspect will be far less engrossing but, perhaps, more useful on a day-to-day basis.

Best wishes,
Frank Stewart

Fulworth
16 April 1914

My Dearest Holmes,

I am aware of the foolishness of writing this letter but I have been without you for nearly two years and I find myself needing some outlet for my emotions. I will destroy these words once I have purged them from my system and you will never know that I did something so helplessly sentimental and foolish.

The last time we were separated for this long was before we had become intimate, when I thought we would remain apart until the next life. I found it nigh on impossible then to get through a day—an hour!—without thinking of you and it has only become harder since then. You have come to be a part of me and I do not function well without you, as I wouldn't without an arm or a leg. Or a heart.

I can hear your scoffings as if you were here now, reading this over my shoulder. No matter. I have not allowed you to quash my 'overbearingly sentimental nature' thus far, and I will not now.

Besides, we both know you are secretly fond of my occasional moments of romanticism, as long as I do not indulge more often than once a week. You scoff with disapproval and speak of the benefits of a rational mind, but I know the soft look in your eye and the twitch of your mouth.

Oh, Holmes, I miss you so much!

If I was truly able to write a letter to you, if you weren't living as another man, if the world would allow me to set my true feelings down without risk of imprisonment, if you wouldn't view such a thing as a terrible waste of paper, what then would I write?

You would want to hear about your hives. They are more than fine, Holmes, I believe they are flourishing. They have grown on me considerably since you first went away. Partially, I suspect, because of the strong association in my mind between you and them, but there is also a primitive, superstitious part of my mind that thinks that as long as I keep your bees in good health, you will return to me with the same.

Perhaps that downplays the matter. I am now able to read the apiology books in your collection with genuine interest, rather than resenting the use of my time in such a manner. I have befriended a fellow bee-keeper with whom I am able to enjoy long conversations on the topic. When you return, I look forward to having similar conversations with you. I think I finally understand your interest in the minutiae of the science.

Your brother has insinuated to me that all is going well with your mission and that you hope to bring this to a close in good time. 'In good time' will likely be far longer than I want it to be, but I am continually hopefully that I will receive word soon that you are on your way back to me.

The first thing I will do when you come back, and when the door is safely locked behind you, will be to kiss you. I think I miss that more than any of the other acts we engaged in together, although not as much as just sitting by the fire and talking to you. Then I will take you up to our room and endeavour to demonstrate just how much I have missed you, and ached for you, without resorting to words. You would only deride those, but you have always held a deep respect for the things I have communicated to you with my body.

I shall definitely have to burn this now. I suppose it just remains for me to tell you the obvious truth you deduced long before I was aware of it, that I love you, and that I wish you safely home to me as soon as may be possible.

Yours always,
John Watson

*

Post Office Telegram
27 July 1914
From: M Holmes, London
To: J Watson, Fulworth
YOUR ASSISTANCE REQUESTED AT HARWICH ON 2ND AUGUST COLLEAGUE REQUIRES A

CHAUFFEUR WOULD PREFER ONE WITH A FAMILIAR FACE

Post Office Telegram
27 July 1914
From: J Watson, Fulworth
To: M Holmes, London
THANK GOD WILL BE THERE

*

The Diary of John H Watson
8 August 1914

Amidst all the emotion of having Holmes home, one memory stands out from today that I will always treasure.

No, that is incorrect. There are several moments I will treasure, not least the bright look in his eye when he first saw our cottage again, the one that told me how much he had missed it. He locked the door with great care, long fingers stroking over the key. When he finally took me in his arms, passion overcame us as we allowed our lips to touch after so long, so much so that I am afraid we committed an act on the living room sofa that the housekeeper would be horrified to know about. He stayed curled up close to me afterwards, as if reluctant to let go. Just holding him there was enough to soothe over the hole inside me that had been formed by the long years of missing him.

We drank a cup of tea together, but Holmes gulped his down rather quickly and then insisted on heading out to the hives to inspect my care of them. There followed a very tense few minutes during which he carefully checked on each hive in silence before finally turning to me.

I braced myself for censure. Holmes has never been retiring about letting me know when I have done a bad job with a task he has set me.

Instead, he gave me a beaming look of pride. "I don't believe I could have looked after them better myself."

I must confess to a rather emotional response to that. It is one thing to be proud of your abilities and quite another when someone you love, and who has a far greater knowledge of the subject, compliments you on them. I kissed him, right there in the sunlight, and he must have still been caught up in the joy of being home, because he kissed me back just as fervently.

Of course, he is still Holmes, so he then rather spoiled the moment by saying, "I take it that Stewart was of as much assistance to you as I anticipated he would be?"

I gave him an expression that made him huff out a laugh. "I told Stackhurst to wait until you were tearing your hair out with frustration before suggesting him as an advisor. I thought you'd need a bit of a push before contacting him."

He is very lucky that I am so overjoyed to have him back with me that it is drowning out any feelings of irritation or anger that I might have felt at the revelation. It did, however, stop me from having any concern at his reaction to the state his apiology books and notes are currently in. Frankly, his 'carefully constructed filing system' can go hang. I was the one having to use them and sorting them by the alphabet made far more sense than whatever peculiar method was behind the apparently random order they were in when he left.

I wonder what his reaction will be when he finds the notes I have added to the margins of some of the more obtuse volumes. I rather look forward to that.

*

First draft of the foreword to the 1920 edition of The Practical Handbook of Bee Culture

There was a time when Holmes asking me to write the foreword for this latest edition of *The Practical Handbook of Bee Culture* would have been a cause for laughter. I must confess to not always being a lover of bees, particularly not as they seemed to home in on me as a prime target for stinging. However, there was a period of just over two years in which Holmes was away from home, during which time I was tasked with looking after his hives.

It was not a task I relished to start with, but as time passed I became increasingly fascinated by these complicated creatures. Their devotion to their work drew me in until I felt as strongly about it as they appeared to, particularly when I was able to share in the fruits of it. Their soaring flights reminded me of the artistry of music and I grew to enjoy watching their delight in it while, naturally, keeping my distance for fear of their sting.

When Holmes returned, he took back control of his hives and I was able to watch a master bee-keeper at work, now with enough understanding to truly appreciate his researches and investigations. This book is the fruit of those investigations and this edition contains some invaluable updates that any man who has learnt to appreciate the singular art of apiology will treasure.

Honey Fuck
By Atlin Merrick

honey fuck (noun): a gentle, romantic act of sexual intercourse

Do bees have a sense of smell?

John Watson wonders a lot of things and that's one of the things about which he wonders.

He's always meant to ask Sherlock about it, but every time the thought pops into his head, Sherlock's doing something more important. Once it was wading hip deep through sewage after some disgustingly floaty evidence. Another time he was buzzing busily about a crowded crime scene. Most recently he was humming contentedly as he sucked John off and, frankly, none of these seemed appropriate instances in which to veer into talk of bees.

Still, John does sometimes wonder and, awake in the still and silent hour of five a.m., he was wondering now.

The reason for this was that John Watson was pretty sure he was nose deaf right now, as in couldn't smell a thing, not one thing. John looked at the man snoring open-mouthed beside him. Specifically he could not smell a *Sherlock* thing.

Because for John this proof still needed proving, the good doctor shifted toward his sleeping beauty and carefully pressed his nose against Sherlock's neck, breathing deep.

No scent.

This was post-case Sherlock Holmes, mind. Sweat-laced, adrenaline-dusted, *John I was only in that skip for ten seconds at most* Sherlock. So on his skin there had

217

to be *something.*

John snugged closer, gently lifted his sweetheart's sleep-boneless arm. He poked his nose into the furry patch beneath, breathed deep.

Nothing.

Grunting his discontent John burrowed deeper, sniffed harder.

Nope.

A third time for luck and a flick of the tongue.

Zilch.

John wriggled closer and, with no ceremony whatsoever, nudged his nose right into Sherlock's half-open mouth. Though he felt the wet heat of breath, there was no smell of last night's garlic risotto or the morning's, well, *morning.*

John did not like this.

Still, there was one part of Sherlock that was always...Sherlocky. It was John's favourite place to experience his sweetheart's scent, a place that was a jumble of comforting, arousing, primal, and potent.

John wriggled slowly, shifted carefully, until he was down between warm, wide-spread thighs.

Pressing his nose to short curls, opening his mouth to maximise surface area, John took a deep, deep breath. No...Sherlocky.

John moved a bit to the left. Nothing. The right. More of the same. Below warm balls, crease of thigh, and he was probably about to give up on any semblance of subtlety entirely and burrow deep down into arse cheeks when there came a sleep-rough rumble. "What are you nosing for down there, John Watson?"

Huffing like a sad dog, John mourned, "I can't smell you." Pillowing his cheek on Sherlock's thigh, he added softly, as if it were a sweet secret. "I can always smell you Sherlock. I can feast on the scent of you even fresh from the bath."

Sherlock is personally fastidious, from well-scrubbed skin to each highly-polished Sutor Mantellassi. Yet since puberty, whether bathed or sweaty, in bed or a cab, dressed in t-shirt or from foot to chin in suit, pretty much the moment Sherlock becomes aroused he smells *horny.*

Which was a problem in the days when the only horns Sherlock wanted to be astride were the kind attached to a dilemma.

Then there was John, who did what others had done—he noticed. Then John did what no one else had done—he made Sherlock care. Because *John* cared. John cared with a hungry, *physical* passion.

A passion that had him again poking his nose at warm, downy short hairs and saying, "You always smell so good, so you, so everything I want, but I can't smell you now."

Sherlock raised himself up on elbows. "Why?"

*

They'd almost closed the case, it was nearly done and dusted, yet Sherlock wanted a quick look around the victim's house. Lestrade thought it unnecessary but gave the go-ahead so long as they took along a pair of constables.

One of whose life John probably saved after the good doctor walked into an airing cupboard back behind the kitchen…and the bee swarm inside it.

"Get away!" he'd shouted, slamming the cupboard door behind him, "Mysliwiec is allergic to bee stings, is he—ouch! fuck!—away?"

Later John found out that DC Grace Superior had

literally picked DC Josef Mysliwiec right on up, carrying him out of the house. At the time all John knew was that he was waiting, waiting, waiting to hear—

"All clear John, get out of there!"

He did. He'd been stung eighteen times.

*

John snuffled at Sherlock's crotch some more. "Because I itched so much I finally took that prescription antihistamine."

John wriggled lower between Sherlock's thighs, hiked up and spread one lean leg, shoved his nose in the crux and sniffed. "Temporary side effect the doctor said, but…"

John pressed his entire face against Sherlock's cock and balls, the lightly furred flesh of perineum.

"…I miss you *today.*"

Sherlock stretched languid. "So use another sense," he said, voice gone husky-low. "Touch me, John. Make me wet." Sherlock reached under the duvet, threaded fingers through John's hair. "Then make yourself wet with me."

Arousal begets arousal. The more Sherlock murmured, the hotter John's breath against Sherlock's thigh, the wider Sherlock's legs went, the more John saw a sexual banquet drowsily waiting to be eaten.

Well, then.

In the spirit of horny enquiry, John swiped a spit-slick tongue along the tender crease at leg and groin. In response, Sherlock placed palms flat on his own thighs, holding himself open.

Laughing giddy, John pulled the duvet high over his head. It would be too hot for Sherlock in minutes, too hot for John much sooner than that…and that was the point.

Make me wet.

Can you will yourself to sweat? Can you?

Sherlock thinks you can.

You can if you start breathing heavy even before your heart kicks up high, you can if you a little bit struggle against your own strength as you spread yourself wide. You can if you concentrate on every part of you touched by every part of *him.*

Barely seconds later and already John felt the heat beneath the duvet climb. He felt his cheeks pinking and his breath washing back against his face as he nipped soft at the knuckles of one of Sherlock's staying hands, then the other.

He loves this, does John, when one of them offers, opens, says *take, please take.*

So John took. He wriggled down, pressed his nose against Sherlock's arse and the hot moistness of the skin there. Sherlock was sweating now, he was getting wet.

Heart thrumming, John licked slow and slower near that humid seam and, like arousal, heat begat sweat begat sighs. He nibbled at balls, at the temptingly delicate skin of thigh, and over and over John felt Sherlock's strong hands keeping himself, keeping himself, keeping himself *open.*

Then John got himself a teasing idea.

Sometimes, if he wants to make Sherlock squirm, John'll suck just one of a thing. One nipple, a single earlobe, a finger, leaving the rest of him untouched. Before long John feels Sherlock's muscles gathering tense and twitchy, springs desperate for the strange release of *symmetry.*

Knowing it would key him up, make him sweat, John nibbled and sucked, licked and nosed now at one hip bone, one bollock, one thigh. He hummed, he tenderly teethed, he slicked Sherlock with spit...but just one, only one, until Sherlock was grunting, twisting his body so that lonesome hipbone-ball-thigh were pressed against John's cheek.

But John was having none of it, so when he pulled back he felt Sherlock's body yearning up and beneath that blanket the wet heat climbed.

"John," Sherlock said, voice gone to gravel, again trying to mate forsaken body parts with inquisitive mouth. Then Sherlock forgot all about symmetry when he felt John's tongue touch a body part of which he very much has only one.

"Wet," John murmured, there under the heavy duvet, "Do you want me to make you wet Sherlock, right..." John swiped his tongue across Sherlock's tight-closed hole. "...right..." He lapped again, slower. "...here?"

John and Sherlock can count on one hand the number of times they've crawled into bed, had a quick fuck, and gone to dreams.

What they cannot count is how often they've done this. Dragged sex out, just damn well made an elaborate spur-of-the-moment who-knows-where-this-is-going *feast* of it.

It's called a honey fuck, a term John probably picked up in med school or the army or maybe somewhere else entirely. No matter where it was from, its meaning was for them simply this: sex that honey-slow, desire met with desire, lust combined with love. Sometimes it came with a side of revelation, possibly confession, but it was always about pleasure, unashamed.

"Yes John," Sherlock whispered way up there, out

in the cool. "Softer John. Slower. Make me ache."

So slower John went, because they could do this a good long while, could Sherlock Holmes and John Watson. Dawdle themselves to blushes, nibble themselves to hard-ons, taking the long way round to what John could feel now: trembling thighs, an almost-but-not-enough turning into nearly-too-much.

And finally came the reward.

A single bead of sweat trickling from the crease of Sherlock's thigh. Meandering moist and salty past his bollocks, it zig-zagged along the path of faint hairs, was nearly to his arse, almost to John's busy tongue, except…John didn't lick.

Instead he pressed his cheek to Sherlock's arse cheek, smeared that sweat against his skin, his nose, his mouth, and he *laughed.*

Sherlock rumbled back, begging, "Tell me."

Like everything else in his world, sex was never *simple* for Sherlock. It was always more than rutting and coming, there were *lessons* to be learned here, as everywhere. For the world's only consulting detective, pleasure fed body *and* brain. "Tell me what's happening, John, Johnny, my John."

John sucked a finger wet, stroked it slowly between the cheeks of Sherlock's arse. Sherlock arched a little, sweated a lot, and John wallowed in that wetness, nose and lips and forehead, murmuring, "Sweat…is different…depending on where it's from." John swiped his tongue beside that wriggling finger until another bead of sweat and another ran fast between Sherlock's legs.

"The eccrine sweat glands on your forehead and palms make a thin, salty perspiration." Here John stopped stroking, stopped licking. "While the apocrine

223

glands at your armpits and genitals produce a heavier, muskier sweat."

The stop-start-stop had Sherlock mumbling, moaning, then arching his back and sliding a foot down John's back. "Please," he said, voice pleasure-slurred. "More."

More *what* Sherlock did not say, so John gusted a hot breath across his sweetheart's cock and said, "Not yet." Because if John couldn't smell Sherlock, well, he was going to take what he could *get*, and what he could get was the sweat of him, the *wet* of him, the damp *mess* of him.

So John made a mess, licking low again, sucking on the soft skin of balls and, graceless giddy, John rubbed-smeared sweat *everywhere*. He blinked butterfly kisses over a slick cock until his lashes were wet. He licked and couldn't taste but licked anyway because it made Sherlock open wider, hump up into his face, mumble needy nonsense.

When John shivered as perspiration trickled down the back of his neck, the consulting genius *deduced* the presence of that perspiration, reached under the duvet to slick his hand through it, then made a noisy production of sucking the sweat from his fingers.

And that officially became enough of that.

Sherlock pushed the duvet away, the sudden chill peaking nipples and raising gooseflesh. He slid his hand down his throat and chest, collecting moisture, then took hold of his cock. "Nownow*now,*" he insisted, yet when John rose onto hands and knees Sherlock put a foot against his chest.

"No."

Nothing happened for exactly as long as necessary to spike the tension.

Then Sherlock rose onto his elbow and said, "I want you to watch me come."

He started to stroke.

A dozen things usually fly fleet through Sherlock's ever-whirring mind. He can, will, and has worked six cases at once while chasing down two more. He'll tinker with three experiments, plan a fourth, and write up the recently-finished fifth. Sometimes, when he's feeling especially dervish, he'll listen to a radio, a television show, the chatter along Baker Street, and Mrs. Hudson singing, a drowning cacophony under which he's alert and distracted both.

But right now Sherlock's brain and his body were exactly where they were and nowhere else: in bed with John.

So the only thing Sherlock listened for was John's breathing, the only thing he watched in pale morning light was John's open mouth, the pulse at his neck. What he tasted was sweat as he tongued the tiny beads above his lip, wondering how it would feel if John did that too, right there and at the same time, his tongue licking beside Sherlock's.

Of all the things that had aroused him since he opened his eyes to soft nuzzling, this was what spiked his adrenaline, and though John couldn't smell him, my my my, Sherlock could certainly smell himself.

When he's in rut Sherlock whiffs of a sweet sort of sweat, thick and heavy. It smells good even to him, it skips his heart faster, makes spit pool under his tongue. He may not have wanted anything to do with fucking before, but that was before John, before John's response to *him*.

Now Sherlock has a conditioned reflex to his own scent. When he's turned on he watches avid, waiting for

John's smile to quirk up, his gaze to drop low, and even after a half dozen years of this Sherlock hasn't grown tired of how arousal begets arousal and so…

…propped on one elbow Sherlock's mouth quirked up, his gaze dropped down, and he watched John's cock thicken and grow wet there, just there, a perfect pearl at the tip.

"Make yourself wet," Sherlock said, then stared *there,* in case wet with *what* wasn't clear.

So, here's a thing: sometimes, just sometimes, John Watson does as he is told.

A soldier learns that lesson quick-smart, his first day in barracks. The lesson continues to be drummed in, week after month after year. No matter how high a man moves he'll always know his place in the chain of command, always know when to *do as he is told.*

Sometimes, just sometimes, John Watson is a soldier again. Sometimes he craves the certainty of order, of *being* ordered.

So John looked at his own erection, saw the drop of pre-come, reached for that heavy drop, collected it a second before it fell, thick and honey-slow.

"Yes," Sherlock whispered, stroking faster. "That," he begged and ordered both. "On *you.* "

John wanted to put his finger in Sherlock's mouth, but those were not his orders, so instead he smeared the pre-come on his own mouth, dabbed it on his cheek, a perfect kind of war paint.

Sherlock reached, clutched the back of John's neck, pulled him to his mouth where he could lick John's lips and chin and cheeks.

He stroked quicker, grunting, mouth and tongue roaming. He made John wet everywhere he could reach, nose and eyelids, neck and collar bones, he fisted his free hand into John's hair and would have started sucking that too, but John rocked back a little and his cock slipped down between Sherlock's legs, poked gently under his balls, and that was it.

Sherlock curled in on himself and came with heavy, slow spurts across his belly.

John watched and so it took longer, as everything that's watched will. By the time Sherlock collapsed onto the bed his entire body shook and his fingernails dug deep into the back of John's neck.

John didn't feel the scrape as Sherlock let go, he *did* feel the chesty rumble of Sherlock's growl and the push of a palm, ordering him *down.*

So down John went and there he made a *mess.*

A mess of cooling come over his chest and hands, a gross, sticky, *laughing* mess because it was good to feel even if he couldn't smell, and it was even better to feel Sherlock twitch ticklish when John's too-long hair brushed his balls.

After that John wasn't laughing, he was stroking himself, encouraged by growls, by the soles of feet rubbing along his back, then by more words though these weren't orders.

"Please," Sherlock said, "here." He pressed flat palms to his belly, slicked three fingers through the wetness still there. When he stuffed them in his mouth, his eyes on John's cock and making *noise,* John came.

The mess he made of Sherlock's belly was warm, it was wet, and that belly, that fine belly, was where John collapsed, boneless, skin a slick mess of everything onto a slick mess of everything and it was there that John Watson passed out cold.

Hours later, after the sun was well and truly risen and the bedroom both hot and bright, the good doctor woke.

The moist, tacky sound flesh made as it unstuck from flesh put John drowsily in mind of that time they did that thing with the buckwheat honey. He was quite possibly about to muse on this memory but instead John Watson frowned. Then he gagged. Then the good doctor got very pushy and very shouty.

"You liar, you little liar!" John shoved Sherlock awake. "You were totally in that skip for more than ten seconds Sherlock Holmes you smell like a rubbish tip you get out of this bed and into the shower this instant oh my god did you *roll* in it get out get out go go go!"

Standing in the shower a minute later, still trying to calm his jangled nerves and his thrumming heart, Sherlock wondered…

Was it wrong to wish John was still nose deaf?

Was it *really?*

It Gets Better
By Wendy C. Fries

Those five near the back? Gay. Those three frowning? Bullied. That one? Oh that one's both.

It's true, John Watson thinks, eyes scanning the two hundred kids assembled in the school gymnasium. If you see you really *can* observe.

John has already done his career-day speech, now Sherlock is standing at the podium finishing his, and John's still surprised Sherlock volunteered them for this.

Then again…John glances at his too-tall, too-thin, too-smart, too-*different* lover. Sherlock knows that for these kids, now, right now, at thirteen, fourteen…it's the most important time in the world.

Sherlock's turned just now, he's looking at him, repeating, "Anything else, John?"

John rises from his chair, goes again to the podium, veers off script. "Just one more quick thing." The doctor looks a long while at as many young faces as he can.

"You *can* do anything. And now is not forever. If you're too short, too skinny, too tall, too fat—" John gestures to himself, "—if you're gay, or think you're gay—" somehow John isn't surprised when Sherlock's hand rests lightly on top of his, "—if you're smart, not-so-smart, or just not sure what you are, please leave here knowing one thing, just this one true thing: It gets better."

John tries again to meet the eye of every single child he's seen slouched, cowed, uncertain, confused.

"I promise you, I promise you on everything I know: *it gets better.*"

Contributors

Amy L Webb (The Love of Apiology) lives in London and has been writing for many years, and a fan of Sherlock Holmes for almost as long. She's greatly indebted to M Quinby for writing Mysteries of Bee-Keeping Explained, which was an invaluable aid in writing this story. twitter.com/Amy_L_Webb.

Anarion (That Escalated Quickly) started writing for the Sherlock fandom when everybody was still posting on LiveJournal and loves writing 221Bs. She is probably best know for her '365 days of 221Bs' challenge. You can find her on LiveJournal at anarion.livejournal.com and on AO3 at archiveofourown.org/users/Anarion/works.

Atlin Merrick (Honey Fuck) is the editor of this book and author of *Sherlock Holmes and John Watson: The Night They Met.* Atlin also writes as Wendy C. Fries. You can find her on social media at Twitter: @atlinmerrick and Tumblr: atlinmerrick.tumblr.com.

Brittany Russ (The One Good Thing To Come Out Of War) My love for writing really became a passion while I was on high school exchange in Japan. The only English literature I had brought with me were my brand new, never before read Sherlock Holmes books. So naturally, as I wrote stories in class to fill the time as the complexity of Chemistry in a foreign language went over my head, they contained Sherlock Holmes and John Watson. I published these stories on LiveJournal, where they were read by the wonderful Atlin. My passions have since moved on from writing, but Atlin is the strongest Muse I have encountered, and the story in this book is the first one I have completed in two years.

Darcy Lindbergh (The Overnight Secret) has been an avid fan of Sherlock Holmes, Dr John Watson, and their adventures--as well as their love story--for many years. She can be found blogging about John and Sherlock, bees, and the occasional dog at watsonshoneybee.tumblr.com.

Elinor Gray (Among the Wildflowers) loves an adventure: in 2014, she moved to London on a whim and spent sixteen months wandering the streets, absorbing the history and living the culture. She considers that time essential research for her queer historical romantic and Sherlock Holmes fanfiction. She has a cat, Zeke, and a yarn stash that is always on the verge of being out of control. Get in touch at elinorgrayauthor.com

Hallie Deighton (Summer) Australian author Hallie Deighton has a master's degree in creative writing, and has been writing longer than she can remember. She is aware that she spent a large proportion of the last four years writing fanfiction under another pseudonym, particularly about BBC's Sherlock. This year she ticked off one of her bucket list items and finally started self-publishing her original work. Hallie currently lives in sunny Queensland with her husband and two kids. When she's not writing, ferrying her children to school and activities or doing the laundry, she works as a librarian. Hallie's original stories can be found at amazon.com/author/halliedeighton.

Jamie Ashbird (A Prodigious Infestation) roams about in her native habitat of Melbourne where she was born, raised, and matured like an excellent Parmesan. And like an excellent Parmesan she is often attacked by her small but vicious cat. She should be writing more, and procrastinating less. @JamieAshbird on Twitter.

Janet A-Nunn (Be Prepared) is an artist/writer, raised in the North of England who now lives in exile in the East Midlands. By day she works in a library, by night she dreams of running away to sea. This is her first published piece, if you discount a prize winning essay about anacondas in her junior school magazine.

Kerry Greenwood (The Secret Diary of Dr John Watson MD) was born in the Melbourne suburb of Footscray and after wandering far and wide, she returned to live there. She is the creator of the Phryne Fisher mystery series of book, on which ABC-TV's *Miss Fisher's Murder Mysteries* is based. Some of Kerry's other works include *The Delphic Women Trilogy: Medea, Cassandra & Electra,* and *Mytherotica.* Kerry has worked as a folk singer, factory hand, director, producer, translator, costume-maker, cook and is currently a solicitor. When she is not doing any of the above she stares blankly out of the window.

Kim Le Patourel (Tales From the River Bank) is an accountant by day, authoress by night—that's what Kim's twitter bio says. Which means she spends a lot of time tapping away frantically on her laptop, writing stories about wars, myths, legends and magic. When she isn't writing or working she reads anything she can lay her hands on, goes to as many theatre productions as she can afford, and walks her beloved Labrador, Marmite, in the woods and fields surrounding her home. You can also find her on twitter, at @kizzia30, where she'll happily chat about anything and everything to anyone who drops by, so please do!

Kimber Camacho (The Case Of The Poison Bees) lives in California and has been married to the same wonderfully talented partner for a surprising number of years. She's been making up stories most of her life; from crayons on construction paper to word processing programs. A voracious reader, Kimber also enjoys a wide variety of music, and has dabbled in other artistic endeavors like drawing and sculpting. She participates in writing-oriented AO3, Dreamwidth, LiveJournal, and Tumblr communities as Random_Nexus. She has had short stories published in anthologies by Circlet Press (circlet.com) and JayHenge Publishing (jayhenge.com), all of which can be found on her Amazon author's page (amazon.com/-/e/B00QSNWX6W).

Kuuttamo (Cover Artist) Kuuttamo describes herself as an artistic, nerdy hippy and passionate Holmesian.

Lucy Jarsdell (The Honeycomb; Little Cupid) is a British librarian, fiction hobbyist, and freelance editor. As well as writing cute romance stories in her free time, she also enjoys tabletop role-playing games, and bakes award winning cakes. She was the first woman in the world to go over Niagara Falls in a Tupperware box. One third of everything she says is completely made up. Watch your step.

Meredith Spies (What's the Buzz?; Prick!) is a writer in the Southeastern United States. She can be found online at facebook.com/meredithaspies or twitter.com/meredithspies. Or both. Both is good. *Prick!* is a "221B", a format of story originated in the online Sherlock fandom in 2008 (KCS/kscribbler is credited as the originator) and follows the style of the story having 221 words, the last one ending in "B," an homage to the Baker Street address of the Victorian (and now modern) dynamic duo. *What's the Buzz* is a little peek into John Watson's thoughts whilst engaged in one of Sherlock's highly suspect investigative techniques. Meredith is a

Sherlock fan from way back and is thrilled to be included in this anthology.

Morgan Black (Becoming) began her professional writing career as a newspaper journalist in Australia. After two country moves and over two decades of working full time in film and television, she now lives in Canada and writes fiction to keep her sanity. She is currently working on a trilogy of mythic fantasy novels set in Celtic Roman Britain. Her forays into all things Sherlockian can be found on A03: archiveofourown.org/users/BlackMorgan and Tumblr: blackmorgan.tumblr.com.

Narrelle M Harris (Nectar; Love Song to a Bee) is an Australian writer of crime, fantasy and romance. Her erotic romance series' include Secret Agents, Secret Lives and the Talbott and Burns Mysteries; her books include the Melbourne-based vampire books The Opposite of Life and Walking Shadows. In Nectar, Narrelle decided, rather than write about bees, to make Sherlock Holmes and John Watson personify the bee (and the flower) themselves, though which is which is up for debate. Follow her on Twitter as @daggyvamp or find out more at narrellemharris.com.

Poppy Alexander (These Things Understood) has been writing transformative and original fiction for over thirty years. She was active in fanzine and mail art culture in the 1980s, haunted rock shows and Goth clubs in the '90s, designed outrageous wigs for club kids in the '00s, and is parenting truly remarkable people in the '10s. She writes every day. PoppyAlexander.com

Stacey Albright (The Stinger) found great joy in the world of Sherlock Holmes and shared that joy with the many new friends she made through it.

Tessa Barding (Bees and Butterflies) has always enjoyed stories, be they written down or put on celluloid, so sooner rather than later she began writing stories, too. In her teens she decided there were films that needed certain adjustments and she embarked on what is now known as fan fiction. Then there was growing up, a job, and writing was put on hold for a while. Then, one day a TV show sparked her interest and here she is, writing once more. Tessa much enjoyed contributing to this anthology and hopes her version of Holmes and Watson is as much fun to read as it was to write.

Verena (The Memory of Bees) usually writes under a pseudonym but thought it would be neat to have one story under her real name that she can show to family and friends.

Verity Burns (A Sting in the Tail) is a writer whose life has been utterly changed by her discovery of Sherlock Holmes. Through Sherlock she met and married her beloved soul mate, and now friends she made through that same Sherlockian connection comfort her as she mourns him. Involvement with Improbable Press is encouraging her to put pen to paper once more!

Wendy C. Fries (It Gets Better) has been a professional writer for more than twenty years and is author of the book *Sherlock Holmes and John Watson: The Day They Met.* Wendy is acquisitions editor for Improbable Press and very much wishes for people to understand, know, *believe* that it does, does, does *get better.* You can find Wendy on social media as Atlin Merrick: Twitter: @atlinmerrick and Tumblr: atlinmerrick.tumblr.com.

The It Gets Better Project

The It Gets Better Project's mission is to communicate to lesbian, gay, bisexual and transgender youth around the world that it gets better, and to create and inspire the changes needed to make it better for them. To learn more about It Gets Better or to donate, go to itgetsbetter.org.

Author and editor profits from *A Murmuring of Bees* are going to supporting the mission of the It Gets Better Project.

Sherlock Holmes and John Watson:
The Night They Met
(19 Ways the World's Most Legendary Love Story
Might Have Begun)

By Atlin Merrick

Some things belong
together, the one with
the other, natural pairs.
    Sherlock Holmes
and John Watson.
Holmes and Watson.
Sherlock and John.
Whether it's in an
empty house during
the Blitz, a West
London strip club in
the 70s, or deep in the
heart of a Hong Kong
computer lab, the
meeting of these two
legendary men is
inevitable.
    Spanning one hundred and twenty-eight years, here
are the stories of that destiny. Of how a detective meets
a doctor, of how they change each other in heart and
mind.
    Of how they fall in love.

Also from Improbable Press

The Adventure of the Colonial Boy
By Narrelle M Harris

1893. Dr Watson, still in mourning for the death of his great friend Sherlock Holmes, is now triply bereaved, with his wife Mary's death in childbirth. Then a telegram from Melbourne, Australia intrudes into his grief: "Come at once if convenient."

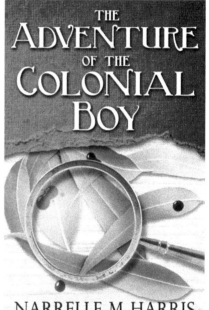

Both suspicious and desperate to believe that Holmes may not, after all, be dead, Watson goes as immediately as the sea voyage will allow. Soon Holmes and Watson are together again, on an adventure through bohemian Melbourne and rural Victoria, following a series of murders linked by a repulsive red leech and one of Moriarty's lieutenants.

But things are not as they were. Too many words lie unsaid between the Great Detective and his biographer. Too much that they feel is a secret.

Solve a crime, forgive a friend, rediscover trust and admit to love. Surely that is not beyond that legendary duo, Sherlock Holmes and Dr John Watson?

Lightning Source UK Ltd.
Milton Keynes UK
UKHW021043050619

343916UK00012B/1280/P

9 780993 513664